Thanking the Lord God on Two Special Occasions

*Eleven Textual Sermons on Thanksgiving Day
and Two Textual Sermons on Church Anniversary Day*

Thanking the Lord God on Two Special Occasions

Eleven Textual Sermons on Thanksgiving Day
and Two Textual Sermons on Church Anniversary Day

DANIEL D. RUPWATE

2019

Thanking the Lord God on Two Special Occasions: *Eleven Textual Sermons on Thanksgiving Day and Two Textual Sermons on Church Anniversary Day:*- published by the Rev. Dr. Ashish Amos of the Indian Society for Promoting Christian Knowledge (ISPCK), Post Box 1585, 1654, Madarsa Road, Kashmere Gate, Delhi-110006.

© Author, 2019

Online Order: http://ispck.org.in/book.php

Also available on amazon.in

ISBN: 978-93-88945-18-9

Cover credit: Internet Sources

Laser typeset at **ISPCK,** Post Box 1585, 1654, Madarsa Road, Kashmere Gate, Delhi-110006.
Tel: 23866323, Fax: 91-11-23865490
e-mail: ashish@ispck.org.in • ella@ispck.org.in
website: www.ispck.org.in

Dedication

This bok is dedicated to Reverend Donald James Foster, (B. A., B. D., M. A.). He was born on August 18, 1930 at Oshawa, Ontario. He attended John English Public School and Mimico High School at Mimico, Ontario. After completing his Matriculation, he attended McMaster University, Hamilton and obtained B. A. in 1954. Then he went to study theology at McMaster Divinity college and obtained B. D. in 1957. During his High School and College years, He was active with Inter-School Christian Fellowship and Inter-Varsity Chritian fellowship. He held the position of President in the McMaster Chapter. He attended Poineer Camp in Muskoka on several occasions. This was an interdenominational organization which brought him in contact with students of other faiths.

At Mimico Baptist Church, he accepted Jesus Christ as Lord and Saviour. He was baptized there. He was preceded into ministry by his two brothers, Rev. Dr. Art Foster of Lenexa, Kansas, U. S. A., and Rev. Charles Foster, Port Perry, Ontario.

He married Shirley Warner at Mimico. They have three children, David, Sharton, and Gary. David is a professor of Political Science at Ashland University at Ashland, Ohio, U. S. A. Sharon lives with her family at Aurora, Ontario. Gary lives with his family in Dundas, Ontario. He works at McMaster University, Hamilton. He helps his father in numerous ways.

Donald and Shirley signed up with Canadian Baptist Overseas Mission Board to serve in India. They spent a year or two with Rev. and Mrs. Gordon Barss at Tekkali, Orisa; and moved to Parlakhemudi, Orissa, to study Oriya language with a tutor. While they were in Larlakhenundi, they supervised a student hostel of twenty high school students. From Parlakhemudi, Rev. Donal Faster made extensive preaching and teaching tours in the Ganjam Malia Association of Baptist Churches using a Willys Jeep on hilly roadways. This was a jungly part of Orissa. They were in Orissa for ten years. They returned to Canada in 1971, for deputational tours.

He went to study at Hartford Seminary Foundation, Hartford, Conn. U. S. A. he wrote a thesis "The Phenomenology of Self-realization: a Study of Vivevakachudamani and Aparokshanubhutti, in 1973.

He joined the McMaster University in 1973 for futher study. The writer of the book met Rev. D. Foster in the same year. They have been close friends since 1973.

Rev. D. Foster complied his correspondence from India to his parents and friends in Candas and published in two volumes. These volumes would guide others how to live in India and serve as missionaries.

The writer asked Rev. D. Foster to edit his books, before they were published. Rev. D. Foster edited the following books.

1. A Biblical Administration of the Church and Society: Nineteen Textual Sermons on Administration of the Church and Fifteen Textual Sermons on Administration of Society, Delhi: ISPCK, 2016

2. The Sanctified, Sacred, and Saved Life of Christians: Twenty-Nine Textual Sermons on Baptism, Marriage, and Funeral Services, Delhi: ISPCK, 2017.

The writer is grateful for the help and friendship of Rev. D. Foster, therefore, he dedicated this book to Rev. Donald James Foster.

Contents

Part - II
Two Textual Sermons on Anniversary Day

Acknowledgments

This book was edited by the Reverend Donald Foster, B. A., B. D., M. A. The author is grateful for his voluntary help and guidance. He has done this favours in case of other books.

The quotations in this book are adopted from the Revised Standard Version, unless otherwise stated.

The picture on the front cover is of a place where the first Thanksgiving service took place. This picture was adopted from internet sources.

Preface

Christians gather together in churches to give thanks to the LORD God on two occasions, namely, Thanksgiving Day and on Anniversary Day of the church. It should be noted that the annual celebration of Thanksgiving Day originated with the settlers in the newly discovered part of the world. Majority of the settlers or pilgrims were from European countries, such as France, Germany, and the Great Britain. Those settlers in the colonies wanted to give thanks to God for their safe arrival in the north America and to thank Him for His providence and protection and for their victory in wars. They also wanted to give thanks to God in Jesus Christ for their religious freedom and for the constitution which gave them freedom to practise their faith and maintain their religious traditions. It should be further noted that the celebration of Thanksgiving Day did not come from the church leaders but it came from the civil authorities, like governors of the States and the Presidents of the United States of America. There are American traditions of Thanksgiving Day, which will be mentioned in the introduction of this book. The writer is not aware of historical traditions of celebrating Church Anniversary Day, he is not able to write about it.

The national Thanksgiving Day and Church Anniversary days are special days in the life of Christians; therefore, they observe these days to thank God in Jesus Christ.

The Presidents of the United States of America declared the Thanksgiving Days in many years. They had religious or pietistic background; therefore they asked their people to celebrate the Thanksgiving Day every year. A few Presidents of the U. S. A. mentioned that the celebration of the Thanksgiving Day were based on Judeo-Christian values. It was their general observation, which is true.

The writer of the book wished to expand the general observation of the Presidents of U. S. A. that celebration of the Thanksgiving Day is based on the biblical values. He planned to select a few texts from the Bible and brought out theological ideas of the texts in order to confirm the conviction of those Presidents of the U. S. A.

The writer applied a similar conviction to the annual celebration of Anniversary Day, which are celebrated by many Christian churches in the U. S.A.

The celebration of the Thanksgiving Day and of Church Anniversary have become universal practices. The writer believes that as all churches celebrate these special days, these occasions gives ministers and preachers to strengthen the biblical values when these values are ignored by secularism in our time.

Rt. Rev. Dr. Daniel D. Rupwate.
Hamiton, Ontario, Canada.

Introduction

A History of Thanksgiving Day

It had been a common tendency among religious people to believe in God and to thank Him for His provisions and protection. This idea is confirmed by seeing that Thanksgiving Day is celebrated in all churches in the world at present. It is celebrated in the churches of the U. S. A., Canada, Britain, Australia, and in the West Indies. It is celebrated in different months and on different Sundays. It has various backgrounds.

We know that the celebration of Mothers' Day, Fathers' Day, and Children's Day originated in the churches of the U. S. A. Similarly, Thanksgiving Day originated in the U. S. A. Thanksgiving Day is a public holiday celebrated on the fourth Thursday of November in the U. S. A. Let us have some information about the origin of the day in the U. S. A.

Thanksgiving Day originated as a harvest festival. It predates the European settlement on North America. Thanksgiving Day was celebrated by Spaniards and the French in 16th century.

Settlers established a colony in Virginia in 1607. They held a thanksgiving in 1610. Thirty-eight English settlers arrived at Berkeley Hundred in Charles city County, Virginia in 1619. This group's London Company charter specifically required "that the day of our ship arrival at the place assigned... in the land of Virginia shall be yearly and perpetually kept holy as a day of thanksgiving to Almighty God."[1]

The Indian Massacre took place in 1622; therefore the colonists abandoned Berkeley Hundred and other locations and moved to Jamestown and other secure places to celebrate Thanksgiving day.

There is another source of celebrating thanksgiving day at Plymouth plantation by the pilgrims. Squanto, a Patuxet Native American, had learned English in his enslavement in England. He moved to America and resided with Wampanoag tribe. He served as interpreter between the pilgrims and the Wampanoag tribe. Massasoit, the leader of the tribe, provided food to the pilgrims during the first winter when supplies brought from England were insufficient. The pilgrims at Plymouth celebrated their first harvest in 1621 three days; this event occurred between September 21 and November 11, 1621. The celebration included 50 pilgrims and 90 Native Americans.[2]

The pilgrims held a true thanksgiving celebration in 1623. After the feast, they had a refreshing 14 day rain which produced a large harvest. William DeLoss Love commented that this thanksgiving was significant because the order to recognize the event was from civil authority, Governor William Bradford (March 19, 1590 – May 9, 1657; Governor 1621-1657), and not from the church, making it the first civil recognition of Thanksgiving in New England. Governor Bradford wrote about the thanksgiving as followed:

> And afterwards the Lord sent them such seasonable showers, with interchange of fair warm weather as, through His blessing, cause a fruitful and liberal harvest, to their no small comfort and rejoicing. For which mercy, in time convenient, they also set apart a day of thanksgiving... By this time harvest was come, and instead of famine now God gave them plenty... for which they blessed God.[3]

There was a controversy over where any 'first thanksgiving' took place. President John F. Kennedy (May 29, 1917 – November 22, 1963; 35th President 1961 – November 22, 1963), in an attempt to strike a compromise between the regional claims, issued Proclamation 3560 on November 5, 1963, stating:

> Over three centuries ago, our forefathers in Virginia and in Massachusetts, far from home in a lonely wilderness, set aside a time of thanksgiving. On

the appointed day, they gave reverent thanks for their safety, for the health of their children, for the fertility of their fields, for the love which bound them together and for the faith which united them with their God."[4]

Thanksgiving was celebrated in the Massachusetts Bay Colony from 1630 and then it became an annual festival since 1680. It was celebrated in the Connecticut Colony in 1639, it became an annual festival after 1647. It was celebrated in the New Netherland Colony since 1644. In the 18th century, individual colonies periodically designated a day of thanksgiving at different times of the year in honour of military victory, on the day of adoption of a state constitution or to celebrated exceptional crop.[5]

During the American Revolutionary war, the Continental Congress appointed one or more thanksgiving days each year; the executives of the various states observed the days in their states.

The first National Proclamation of Thanksgiving was given by the Continental Congress in 1777 from York, Pennsylvania. Samuel Adams (September 27, 1722 – October 2, 1803) drafted the proclamation and the Congress adopted the final version, as followed:

> For as much as it is the indispensable Duty of all Men to adore the superintending Providence of Almighty God; to acknowledge with Gratitude their Obligation to him for Benefits received, and to implore such farther Blessings as they stand in Need of: And it having pleased him in his abundant Mercy, not only to continue to us the innumerable Bounties of his common Providence; but also to smile upon us in the Prosecution of a just and necessary War, for the defense and establishment of our unalienable Rights and Liberties; particularly in that he hath been pleased, in so great Measure, to prosper the Means used for the Support of our Troops, and to crown our Arms with most signal success. It is therefore recommended to the legislative or executive Powers of these United States to set apart Thursday, the eighteenth day of December next, for Solemn Thanksgiving and Praise...[6]

George Washington (February 22, 1732 – December 14, 1999; 1st President 1789 – 1797), who was a leader of revolutionary forces in the American Revolutionary War, proclaimed a Thanksgiving in December 1777 as a victory celebration against the British forces at Saratoga.

The Continental –Confederation Congresss made a proclamation, on November 5, 1782, as followed:

> It being the indispensable duty of all nations, not only to offer up their supplications to Almighty God, the giver of all good, for His gracious assistance in a time of distress, but also in a solemn and public manner, to give Him praise for His goodness in general, and especially for great and signal interpositions of His Providence in their behalf, therefore, the United states in congress assembled, taking into their consideration the many instances of Divine goodness to these States in the course of the important conflict in which they have been so long engaged-..... In appointing and commanding the observance of THURSDAY the TWENTY-EIGHTH DAY OF NOVEMBER next as a day of SOLEMN THANKSGIVING to GOD for all His mercies; and they do further recommend to all ranks to testify their gratitude to God for His goodness by a cheerful obedience to His laws and by promoting, each in his station, and by influence, the practice of true and undefiled religion, which is the great foundation of public prosperity and national happiness.[7]

President George Washington made the proclamation and created the first Thanksgiving Day to be observed by the United States of America. He said:

> Whereas it is the duty of all Nations to acknowledge the providence of Almighty God, to obey his will, to be grateful for his benefits, and humbly to implore his protection and favor, and whereas both Houses of Congress have by their joint Committee requested me "to recommend to the People of the United States a day of public thanksgiving and prayer to be observed by acknowledging with grateful hearts the many signal favors of Almighty God especially by affording them an opportunity peaceably to establish a form of government for their safety and happiness" Now therefore I do recommend and assign Thursday the 26th day of November next to be observed by the People of these States to the service of that great and glorious Being, who is the beneficient Author of all good that was, that is, or that will be.........[8]

George Washington again proclaimed a Thanksgiving in 1795. President John Adams (October 30, 1735 – July 4, 1826; 2nd President 1797 – 1801) declared Thanksgiving in 1798 and 1799. President James Medison (March 16, 1751 – June 28, 1836; 11th President 1809 – 1817) renewed a tradition and declared Thanksgiving in 1814 and in 1815. Then Governor William Plumer (June 25, 1759 – December 22, 1850; Governor 1812 – 1813, 1816 – 1819) of New Hampshired appointed November 14 as a day of Public Thanksgiving in 1816. Governor John Brooks (May 4, 1752 – March 1, 1825, 11th Governor 1816 – 1823) of Massachusetts appointed November 28 as a day of Thanksgiving in 1816. By 1858 the governors of 25 States and two territories proclaimed the day of Thanksgiving.[9]

After the civil war, President Abraham Lincoln (February 12, 1809 – April 15, 1855; 16th President 1861 – 1865) declared to observe Thanksgiving Day, on October 3, 1863, saying:

> It has seemed to me fit and proper that they should be solemnly, reverently and gratefully acknowledged as with one heart and voice by the whole American people. I do therefore invite my fellow citizens in every part of the United States, and also those who are at sea and those who are sojourning in foreign lands, to set apart and observe the last Thursday of November next, as a day of Thanksgiving and Praise to our beneficent Father who dwelleth in the Heavens. And I recommend to them that while offering up the ascription justly due to him for such singular deliverances and blessings, they do also, with humble penitence of our national perverseness and disobedience, commend to his tender care all those who have become widows, orphans, mourners or sufferers in the lamentable civil strife in which we are unavoidably engaged, and frequently implore the interposition of Almighty Hand to heal the wounds of the nation and to restore it as soon as may be consistent with the Divine purposes to the full employment of peace, harmony, tranquility and Union.[10]

Abraham Lincoln's successors as presidents followed his example of annually declaring the last Thursday in November as Thanksgiving Day. President Franklin D. Roosevelt (January 30, 1882 – April 12, 1945; 32nd President 1933 – 1945) broke the tradition in 1939 to 1941. In December 1941, senate passed an amendment to resolution. The amendment also passed the House. Then the President Roosevelt signed a bill, for the first time, making the date of Thanksgiving a matter of federal law as the fourth Thursday of November.[11]

At Thanksgiving Day, poor are provided with food. Many communities have annual food drives, collecting non-perishable packaged and canned foods. Thanksgiving parades take place in many cities.

Although Thanksgiving Day has become a civil holiday, its religious perspective should not be forgotten. Thanksgiving was founded as a religious observance for American community to thank God for a common purpose. They thanked God for safe arrival in the U. S. A.; they thanked God for winning war battle of Saratoga; they thanked God for their civil and religious liberty and for God's Providence. President Washington and President Grover Cleveland (1837 – 1908; 22nd President 1885 – 1889; 24th President 1893 – 1897) expressed a specifically Christian perspective in their declarations. President William McKinley (January 29, 1843 – September 14, 1901; 25th President March 4, 1897 – September 14, 1901) and other Presidents cited the Judeo-Christian tradition.[12] Thanksgiving services are held on the Thanksgiving Day by almost all churches.

Endnotes

[1] *https://en.wipedia.org./wiki/Thanksgiving* (united States) p.1.

[2] *Ibid.*, p.1.

[3] *Ibid.*, p.3.

[4] *Ibid.*, p.4.

[5] *Ibid.*, p.4.

[6] *Ibid.*, pp.4-5.

[7] *Ibid.*, pp.5-6.

[8] *Ibid.*, pp.6-7.

[9] *Ibid.*, p.8.

[10] *Ibid.*, pp.9-10.

[11] *Ibid.*, p.11.

[12] *Ibid.*, p.13.

Part I
Eleven Textual Sermons on Thanksgiving Day

Chapter 1

Titles of the Sermon

'Responsive Gratitude,'

'Thanking God for His Gifts,'

'Thinking of God and Thanking God,'

'Appreciating God's Providence.'

Scripture

Deuteronomy 8:1-20

Exodus 16:13, 15, 16, 31, 35; 23:16

Deuteronomy 8:3, 7-10, 17-20; 16:16-17

Joshua 6:1-21; 5:12; 8:1-29; 10:8,14

Nehemiah 9:21

Psalms 20:7-8; 50:22-23

Matthew 4:4; 7:7-11

II Corinthians 9:6-11

Text: Deuteronomy 8:10

A Few Versions of the Text: Deuteronomy 8:10

When you have eaten and are full, then you shall bless the LORD your God for the good land which He has given you. *New King James Version*

And thou shalt eat and be full, and thou shalt bless Jehovah thy God for the good land which He hath given thee. *The Wesleyan Bible Commentary*

When you have eaten and are satisfied, praise the LORD your God for the good land he has given you. *Revised Standard Version*

When you have eaten and are satisfied, praise the LORD your God for the good land He has given you. *New International Version*

You will have plenty to eat and will bless the LORD your God for the rich land he has given you. *The New English Bible*

When you have eaten your fill, bless the Lord your God for the good land he has given you. *The Living Bible Illustrated*

When you have eaten all you want, thank the LORD your God for the good land he has given you. *God's Word*

Introduction

The second Sunday of December is called "White Gift Sunday." This Sunday is observed in all churches in the world; its universal observance has a traditional or historic significance for the Church. On this Sunday, gifts -clothes, money, grocery items - are collected to be distributed among the poor and the needy. The tradition of bringing gifts in churches on the White Gift Sunday was based on the concept of giving thanks to God for the benefits the believers received at the hands of God. The believers have to think of and recall what God did for them, how God cared for them, how He loved them, how He guided them. This remembrance of God's good deeds for the believers is to be expressed in helping the poor and the needy.

Rev. John Wesley (June 17,1703-March 2,1791), a founder of Methodist Church, used to beg money throughout the United Societies for the poor so that he could distribute food, clothes, coal for them. He appointed seven stewards; and instructed them to help the poor by giving them gifts, by saying words of comfort and encouragement. He appealed rich Methodists to care for the poor brethren and to share their wealth with them, because God gave them riches for this noble purpose.[1]

The Salvation Army came out of Methodist Church. It has concentrated on social services and charitable missions. During December, Salvation Army raises money for the poor and the needy and provide them relief at Christmas and other days. It's noble practice of helping the needy came out of the Methodist Church. The practice was established by Rev. John Wesley; it was mentioned before. The Methodist churches should reemphasise the practice of helping the poor, needy, and the destitute.

Introduction of the Text

All Christian churches observe "Thanksgiving Sunday" on the second Sunday of October in Canada and in other countries in the world. Christian practice or tradition of observing "Thanksgiving Sunday" in all churches in the world can be linked with the commandment, which God gave to the people of Israel, in the following words:

> **When you have eaten and are satisfied, praise the LORD your God for the good land he has given you.** (Deuteronomy 8:10)

This is the text of our meditation now.

The Context of the Text

Through Moses, God was leading the people of Israel to the promised land, wherein there would be plenty of all good things. As the people of Israel came to the boarder of the promised land, Moses exhorted them not to forget God but to thank Him for all the benefits they would receive in the promised land. Moses knew his people Israel very well; he knew the human nature to forget the Benefactor, the LORD God, who had been doing beneficial deeds to the people. Moses wished his people to remember the LORD God and to praise Him, because He led them to the promised land; and He would make them settled in the fertile land. He exhorted the people, saying,

When you have eaten and are satisfied, praise the LORD your God for the good land he has given you. (Deut. 8:10)

This is the text, within its historical and theological background.

An Analysis of the Text

This text has three ideas. (A) The first idea is that God would give the people the good land.

(B) The second idea is that the people would eat and be satisfied with the provisions of the promised land.

(C) The third idea is that the people should praise the LORD God when they have eaten and are satisfied.

Exposition of the Ideas of the Text

(A) The first idea of the text is that God would give the people the good land. Moses told the people of Israel that God would give them the good land as He had promised them. Moses was sure that God would keep His promises at all times. Moses was assured of the promise of God, because he experienced God's grace and goodness while he was leading the people of Israel through the wilderness forty years. He reminded the people that God fed them *manna*, the food which their fathers did not know (Ex. 16:15; Deut. 8:3,16). God supplied the *manna* miraculously; the food was dropped from the sky (Ex. 16:13, 31). God supplied the *manna* until the people were able to cultivate land and produce food for themselves (Ex. 16:35; Jos. 5:12); the people did not lack food while they were passing through the wilderness. God kept His promise to provide food to the people. God proved through the miraculous supply of food that man does not live by bread alone but he lives by the word of God. When Jesus Christ was tempted by the devil, He quoted the scripture to silence the devil (Mt. 4:4) Moses also experienced that God provided plentiful water, plentiful clothing, and plenty of footwear in the wilderness for forty years. These miraculous provisions were referred by Nehemiah (Neh. 9:21). As God was able to provide everything in abundance in the wilderness, where there could be scarcity of basic supply, He would certainly provide every good thing in a good land.

Moses had experienced goodness of the LORD God, therefore, he was convinced that God would give the people of Israel the good land. As God is good, He would confirm His goodness by giving good things to the people who believe in Him. Jesus Christ made this point, in His sermon on the Mount, when He said:

> Ask, and will be given you; seek and you will find; knock, and it will be opened to you. For every one who asks receives, and he who seeks finds, and to him who knocks it will be opened. Or what man of you, if his son asks him for bread, will give him a stone? Or if he asks for a fish, will give him a serpent? If you then, who are evil, know how to give good gifts to your children, how much more will your Father who is in heaven give good things to those who ask him! (Mt. 7:7-11)

In other words, God, who is good by nature, always gives good things to His children.

(B) The second idea of the test is that the people would eat and be satisfied with the provisions of the promised land. The promised land would be a good land. The good land would have plentiful water supply; there would be brooks of water and fountains of water everywhere. The good land would be the fertile land. It would yield wheat and barley abundantly. It would have various fruit-bearing trees, such as, fig trees, pomegranates, and olive trees. The land would have vines, producing grapes to eat and wine to drink abundantly. The land would have minerals, like iron and copper. The land would have everything plentiful (Deut. 8:7-10). Moses told the people that God's promised land would be the land of abundance of every thing.

Moses warned the people of Israel against the possibly wrong attitude toward themselves and toward God when they would possess the promised land and enjoy everything. The people would take pride in themselves and forget the LORD God who gave them the fertile land. Moses exhorted the people in these words:

> Beware lest you say in your heart, 'My power and the might of my hand have gotten me this wealth.' You shall remember the LORD your God, for it is he who gives you power to get wealth; that he may confirm his covenant which he swore to your fathers, as at this day. And if you forget the LORD your God and go after other gods and serve them and worship them, I solemnly warn you this day that you shall surely perish. Like the nations that

the LORD makes to perish before you, so shall you perish, because you
would not obey the voice of the LORD your God. (Deut. 8:17-20)

In other words, Israel should not boast of its power and wealth; but
she has to remember that God has had given her every good thing.

We should note that the promised and the good land was a gift of
God to the people of Israel. They did not conquer the land by their
military power. Let us recall a few events how Israel got the possession
of the promised land.

Jericho was a well-fortified city. People of Israel could not enter
the city. God asked through Joshua the people of Israel to go around
the walls of Jericho seven days. When they circumvented seven times
on the seventh day the wall of the city fell down and Israel was able
to take control of the city. It was an act of God (Jos. 6:1-21).

The people of Israel captured the city of Ai by ambush as God
had asked them to do. (Jos.8:1-29). When the people of Gibeon heard
how Joshua entered cities of Jericho and Ai they submitted themselves
as servants of Israel; and made a peace treaty with Israel. But the king
of Jerusalem Adonizedk asked other kings to jointly fight against Israel.
God told Joshua:

Do not fear them, for I have given them into your hands. There shall not
a man of them stand before you. (Jos.10:8)

God killed those people with hail stones. The sun stayed in the midst
of heaven, so that Israel could kill the people of other nations. It was
God who fought for Israel (Jos.10:14). Joshua was able to capture the
whole land, because God was fighting for Israel. God was fulfilling
His promise to give a good land to Israel. The good land, with all its
prosperity, was a gift of God to Israel.

David was a shepherd but God raised him to be a wealthy and
powerful king. When David achieved a distinction as a powerful and
wealthy king, he kept himself humble before God, because he knew
that he received all things from the hand of God. King David (1002-
962 B. C.) won many victories in wars, yet he knew that God made
him victorious in those wars. He wrote:

> Some boast of chariots, and some of horses; but we boast of the name of
> the LORD our God. They will collapse and fade; but we shall rise and stand
> upright. (Ps. 20:7-8)

(C) The third idea of the text is that the people should praise the
LORD God when they have eaten and are satisfied. When the people
of Israel would be settled in the promised land, and when the good
land would yield every good thing in abundance, and they would enjoy
and be satisfied, they should express their gratitude toward God for
His provisions, care, and concerns. They should praise the LORD
their God.

Moses said it very clearly that the people should worship the LORD
God. This means that Moses put an emphasis on a form of corporate
worship; Moses wished that the community of the faithful should
worship God when they are satisfied with the divine provisions.

There was a religious stipulation as to how every person had to
enter the temple of God. God, through Moses, told the people of
Israel, saying, "No one shall come into my presence empty-handed."
(Ex. 23:16) The same commandment appears in a positive manner,
in these words:

> They shall not appear before the LORD empty-handed; every man shall give
> as he is able, according to the blessing of the LORD your God which he has
> given you. (Deut. 16:16-17)

In these verses, we find the stipulation as to how much an individual
was expected to give to God's work. The giving to God's work has to
be in proportion with God's blessing received by an individual. This
is the way the believers have to praise and worship God. The believers
are expected not to deprive God of His portion and to cheat Him.
They have to worship God with the offerings of thanksgiving. God
spoke through a psalm writer concerning this:

> Mark this, then, you who forget God, lest I rend, and there be none to
> deliver! He who brings thanksgiving as his sacrifice honours me; to him who
> orders his way aright I will show the salvation of God. (Ps. 50:22-23)

St. Paul exhorted Christians in a similar way, when he wrote these words:

> The point is this: he who sows sparingly will also reap sparingly, and he who sows bountifully will also reap bountifully. Each one must do as he has made his mind, not reluctantly or under compulsion, for God loves a cheerful giver. And God is able to provide you with every blessing in abundance, so that you may always have enough of everything and may provide in abundance for every good work. As it is written, 'He scatters abroad, he gives to the poor; his righteousness endures for ever.' He who supplies seed to the sower and bread for food will supply and multiply your resources and increase the harvest of your righteousness. You will be enriched in every way for great generosity, which through us will produce thanksgiving to God. (II Cor. 9:6-11)

An Application and Conclusion

Moses exhorted the people of Israel in the words of the text, "When you have eaten and are satisfied, praise the LORD your God for the good land he has given you." This exhortation is relevant to the Christians, who have entered Canada as immigrants. Canada has become the land of promises and opportunities to majority of the immigrants. They have many reasons to praise God in Christ Jesus, such as, high standard of living, abundance of every thing, peace and order in the land, freedom of religious expression, etc. Therefore, they have to be grateful to God and praise Him with their generous offerings of thanksgiving for the work of God and for caring the poor and the needy in this land and other lands.

Recommended Hymns from the Methodist Hymnal

18   'Let us with a gladsome mind'

64   'Praise to the Lord, the Almighty'

550   'O For a heart to praise my God,'

851   'All things bright and beautiful'

962   'Come, ye thankful people, come'

968   'Yes, God is good- in earth and sky'

Recommended Responsive Reading from the Methodist Hymnal

#29 (p. 395).

Recommended Responsive Reading from *A Worship Manual for Scriptural or Methodist Order of Service*

22 (pp. 106-108).

Endnotes

[1] The Works of John Wesley, (Grand Rapids, Michigan: Baker Book House, Reprinted 1984) Vol. II, p. 59; Vol. IV, p. 295; Vol. VII, p. 286; Vol. I, pp. 309, 455, 458.

Chapter 2

Titles of the Sermon

'Repaying to the LORD God'

'Ingratitude towards God'

'Questionable Way of Requiting the LORD God.'

Scripture

Deuteronomy 31:24-32:22

Genesis 1:26-27; 5:1; 12:2

Exodus 19:3-6

Deuteronomy 7:1-2; 31:10-11; 32:29

Joshua 23:3-6

II Samuel 7:23-24

Nehemiah 9:26-27,29

Job 33:4

Psalms 8:5-8; 27:5, 10; 100:3

Proverbs 1:7; 12:15; 13:19; 15:12

Romans 1:18-23, 26-32

Text: Deuteronomy 32:6

A Few Versions of the Text, Deuteronomy 32:6

Do you thus deal with the LORD, O foolish unwise people? Is He not your Father, who bought you? Has He not made you and established you? *The New King James Version*

Do you thus requite Jehovah, O foolish people and unwise? Is not he thy father that hath bought thee? He hath made thee, and established thee. *The Wesleyan Bible Commentary*

Do you thus requite the LORD, you foolish and senseless people? Is not he your father, who created you, who made you and established you? *Revised Standard Version*

Is this the way you repay the LORD, O foolish and unwise people? Is he not your Father, your Creator, who made you and formed you? *New International Version*

Is this how you repay the LORD, you brutish and stupid people? Is he not your father who formed you? Did he not make you and establish you? *The New English Bible*

Is this the way you treat Jehovah? O foolish people, Is not God your Father? Has he not created you? Has he not established you and made you strong? *The Living Bible Illustrated*

Is this how you repay the LORD, you foolish and silly people? Isn't he your Father and Owner, who made you and formed you? *God's Word*

Introduction

There are some thanksgiving services in the Bible. Those services were held, when kings and the people of Israel realized and recognized with what and how God blessed them. The intent of those thanksgiving services was to thank God for the benefits they received at God's hand, and to praise God by acts of thanksgiving sacrifices and freewill offerings. However, people forgot God to thank Him several times. Therefore, the people were reminded of the divine benefits so that they may return to God and keep His commandments, and practise holiness and righteousness in their daily life.

When the people are rich or affluent, they tend to forget God and they do not thank Him, because they take God's blessings granted.

(1) This is a story about forgetting God to thank Him for His blessings. Alfonso XII (November 28,1857-November 25, 1885) was a good king of Spain. He came to know that the pages at his court forgot to ask God's blessing on their daily meals. The king wanted to rebuke the pages and correct their attitude.

The king invited the pages for a banquet. The table was spread with every kind of good things. The boys ate the feast. But none of them remembered to ask God's blessing on the food.

While the feast was going on, a beggar entered the banquet hall; he was wearing dirty clothes. He sat at the royal table and ate and drank to his heart content. The boys were surprised to see the beggar dinning at the royal table; they expected the king would order him to go away. But the king said nothing.

The beggar finished his dinner and rose from the table and left the boys and the king without saying a word of thanks.

The boys were offended much; they could not keep silence any longer. They said: "What a despicably mean fellow!" Then the king said to the boys, "Boys, bolder and more audacious than this beggar have you all been. Every day you sit down to a table supplied by the bounty of your Heavenly Father, yet you ask not His blessing nor express to Him your gratitude. [1]

(2) This is an event which took place in the life of a small congregation. The congregation was financially poor. Nevertheless, the congregation decided to support a person to go abroad for being trained to be a missionary. The person finished her training. After the training, the congregation was expecting of her to visit the church and give report about her training. But she disappointed the congregation. What the congregation would have felt about her whom they supported financially in the past? She had no sense of gratitude toward that small congregation; therefore, she ignored the congregation and never said a word of thanksgiving.

Introduction of the Text

It is not right to forget to thank God and man for benefits received from them. To show ingratitude is morally wrong. The Bible does not approve this wrong attitude toward God. Moses, who was instrumental to liberate the people of Israel from Egyptian bondage, said to the people about this wrong attitude, in the following words:

> Do you thus requite the LORD, you foolish and senseless people? Is not he your father, who created you, who made you and established you? (Deut. 32:6)

This is the text of our meditation now.

The Context of the text

The words of the text are taken from the song, which was composed by Moses. Moses composed the song, when he wrote down the law of God. He commanded the priests and the elders of Israel to read the law during the Feast of Tabernacle (Deut. 31:10-11). Moses also gave his poem to the priests for a specified purpose.

Secondly, the death of Moses was approaching and he had to hand over leadership to Joshua. God told Moses that the people of Israel would forget what He did for them. They would rebel against Him. They would suffer from crises, because of their wickedness. Moses was inspired to write the poem. Moses gave the poem to the priests that they may recite the poem for the people of Israel so that the poem may stand as a witness against the people of Israel. The intent of the poem is expressed in the words of the text:

> Do you thus requite the LORD, you foolish and senseless people? Is not he your father, who created you, who made you and established you? (Deut. 32:6)

This is the text within its historical setting.

An Analysis of the Text

This text has three ideas. (A) The first idea is a question to the people of Israel, "Do you thus requite the LORD?

(B) The second idea is that their way of repaying the LORD made them to be foolish and senseless people.

(C) The third idea comprises two questions about their creation and establishment as the people of God with reference to God: (i) "Is not He your father, who created you, who made you and (ii) established you?

Exposition of the Ideas of the Text

Let us deal with the third idea of the text first, because it talks about God as the creator of the people of Israel, who established them. The first idea of the text is a question of how the people of God should repay Him. The second idea is a judgment on the way the people dealt with God. This is a logical way of dealing with the ideas in sequence.

(C) The third idea of the text consists of two questions: (i) Is not God your father, who created you, who made you and (ii) established you? In other words, the questions are: Is God not the Father of the people of Israel, who created them? And Has God not established them as His people? The answers to these rhetorical questions are positive, i.e., God is the Father of the people of Israel, who created them and God established them as His people.

The people of Israel believed that the LORD God is their creator and they are His people. A psalmist, in a psalm for the thanks offering, expressed this belief in the following words:

> Know that the LORD is God! It is he that made us, and we are his; we are his people, and the sheep of his pasture. (Ps. 100:3)

The belief, that God is the creator and the spiritual Father of the people of Israel, extends beyond race of Israel; it embraces all mankind. This is a fundamental creed of the Bible. The creation story, recorded in the Bible, tells us that man is made or created in the image of God:

> Then God said, 'Let us make man in our image, after our likeness... So God created man in his own image, in the image of God he created him; male and female he created them. (Gen. 1:26-27; cf. Gen. 5:1; Job 33:4; Ps. 8:5-8)

God created man in His image, a special being among all other beings. He created man not of a necessity, but out of love. He had been expressing His love to mankind by caring, protecting, and establishing them. God cares for His person more than the parents of the person. King David expressed this tested belief in the following words:

> For he will hide me in his shelter in the day of trouble; he will conceal me under the cover of his tent, he will set me high upon a rock. (Ps. 27:5)... For my father and my mother have forsaken me, but the LORD will take me up. (Ps. 27:10)

The second question is: And Has God not established them as His people? Yes, He did so. God promised Abram that He would make a great nation out of him (Gen. 12:2). In keeping with His promise, God liberated the people of Hebrews from the Egyptian bondage. Then God spoke to the people of Hebrews, through Moses, in these words:

> Thus you shall say to the house of Jacob, and tell the people of Israel: You have seen what I did to the Egyptians, and how I bore you on eagle's wings and brought you to myself. Now therefore, if you will obey my voice and keep my covenant, you shall be my own possession among all people; for all the earth is mine, and you shall be to me a kingdom of priests and a holy nation. (Ex. 19:3-6)

God established the people of Israel as a mighty nation. In order to do it, God cleared away many nations such as Hittites, Girgashites, Amorites, Hivites, and Jebusites, before Israel. Those nations were greater and mightier than Israel (Deut. 7:1-2 Cf. II Sam. 7: 23-24). Under the leadership of Joshua, the promised land became the country of the people of Israel. Joshua in his address to the elders, judges and officers, said:

> I am now old and well advanced in years; and you have seen all that the LORD your God has done to all these nations for your sake, for it is the LORD your God who fought for you. Behold, I have allotted to you as an inheritance for your tribes these nations that remain, along with all the nations that I have already cut off, from the Jordan to the Great Sea in the west. The LORD your God will push them back before you, and drive them out of your sight; and you shall possess their land, as the LORD your God promised you. Therefore be very steadfast to keep and do all that is written in book

of the law of Moses, turning aside from it neither to the right hand nor to the left. (Jos. 23:3-6)

God was the Father of the people of Israel. He created a nation for them; He carved a nation for them in the face of fierce opposition; and He established them as a mighty nation.

(A) The next idea of the text is a question to the people of Israel, "Do you thus requite the LORD? In other words, Moses asked the people of Israel, "Do you thus repay to the LORD, the creator and establisher of them? God did all good things for the people of Israel; therefore, Moses expected of the people to remember God as the caring Father. God foretold Moses that the people of Israel would forget the LORD God; and they would leave Him and go after other gods; they would break God's covenant (Deut. 31:16). They would commit sins against the holy God; they would act corruptly; therefore, they would kindle the wrath of God against them (Deut. 32:29). When God foretold how the people would forget Him and how they would commit sins against the LORD God, Moses exhorted the people not to act this way, because it would be morally wrong to pay back evil for good.

What the LORD God foretold to Moses came to pass. The history of the people of Israel is full of events narrating how they sinned against God and how God punished them. When they repented of the evil, God forgave their sins, and showed His mercy to them. Reflecting on the history of Israel, Nehemiah wrote:

> Nevertheless they were disobedient and rebelled against thee and cast thy law behind their back and killed thy prophets, who had warned them in order to turn them back to thee, and they committed great blasphemies. Therefore thou didst give them into the hand of their enemies, who made them suffer; and in the time of their suffering they cried to thee and thou didst hear them from heaven; and according to thy great mercies thou didst give them saviours who saved them from the hand of their enemies... And thou didst warn them in order to turn them back to thy laws. Yet they acted presumptuously and did not obey thy commandments, but sinned against thy ordinances, by the observance of which a man shall live, and turned a stubborn shoulder and stiffened their neck and would not obey. (Neh. 9:26-27, 29)

The Lord God had been revealing Himself to the Gentiles, non-Jews, His holy laws. He punished them for the sins, which they committed against the limited divine revelation to the Gentiles. St. Paul wrote about this spiritual fact to the Christians at Rome, in these words:

> For the wrath of God is revealed from heaven against all ungodliness and wickedness of men who by their wickedness suppress the truth. For what can be known about God is plain to them, because God has shown it to them... So they are without excuse; for although they knew God they did not honour him as God or give thanks to him, but they became futile in their thinking and their senseless minds were darkened. Claiming to be wise, they became fools, and exchanged the glory of the immortal God for images resembling mortal man or birds or animals or reptiles. (Rom. 1:18-23)

Then St. Paul added that because of dishonouring God, they were committing all kinds of evil deeds (Rom. 1:26-32). God punished the Jews and the Gentiles for breaking His holy laws. The response of the people toward God's holy laws was wrong.

(B) The final idea of the text is that the way of the people to thus repay the LORD made them to be foolish and senseless people. In other words, the people of Israel did not respond to God's fatherly love and care in a wise and sensible way. On the contrary, they acted foolishly and senselessly.

The Bible classifies foolishness and senselessness as opposite of wisdom and understanding. Foolishness does not mean lack of intelligence. It rather means the tendency to do against what is right and good or to do wrong and evil. The scripture has spoken about foolishness many times, in this way:

> The fear of the LORD is the beginning of knowledge; fools despise wisdom and instruction. (Pr. 1:7)

Again,

> The way of a fool is right in his own eyes, but a wise man listens to advice. (Pr. 12:15)

The scripture considers the foolishness as a cause of evil action. It says, "but to turn away from evil is an abomination to fools." (Pr. 13 19) It adds that a fool enjoys his foolishness. He has no desire to do what is right, as these words state: "Folly is a joy to him who has no sense, but a man of understanding walks aright. " (Pr. 15:12) St. Paul reaffirmed this idea, when he wrote:

> For although they knew God they did not honor him as God or give thanks to him, but they became futile in their thinking and their senseless minds were darkened. Claiming to be wise, they became fools. (Rom. 1:21-22)

These words were quoted before in explaining the previous idea.

God chose the people of Israel to be His people for the purpose of propagating the knowledge of God in the world. He revealed His knowledge and wisdom to them through prophets, priests, and poets that they be wise people and making the world wise. But the people of Israel ignored God's revelation; they disobeyed God and broke His commandments. They knew the word of God; yet they sinned against God. God punished them for their iniquities many times; but they did not change their way of responding to God appropriately.

Conclusion

Moses reminded the people of Israel that God created them and made them His chosen people. He carved a mighty nation of Israel in the face of more powerful nations than Israel. He delivered them from all dangers and showed His mercy to them. God faithfully kept His covenant and promise with the people of Israel. He cared for them and He established them as a nation. Yet they forgot God and worshipped other gods. They acted foolishly and wickedly. God punished them for their sins. From this spiritual history of Israel, believers have to learn how to respond to God's love and care wisely and responsibly. This was the intention of the exhortation of Moses to the people of Israel and to us now.

Recommended Hymns from the Methodist Hymnal

10   'Now thank we all our God'

12   'Praise my soul, the King of heaven,'

64   'Praise to the Lord, the Almighty'

550   'O For a heart to praise my God'

851   'All things bright and beautiful,'

963   'We plough the fields, and scatter'

968   'Yes, God is good- I earth and sky,'

969   'O LORD of heaven and earth and sea'

Recommended Responsive Reading from the Methodist Hymnal

61 (p. 411)

Recommended Responsive Reading from *A Worship Manual for Scriptural or Methodist Order of Service*

59 (pp.161-163).

Endnotes

[1] Paul Lee Tan, Encyclopedia of 7700 Illustrations: Signs of the Times, Rockville, Maryland: Assurance Publishers, Nineth Printing, 1985) # 4660.

Chapter 3

Titles of the Sermon
'Cheerful Thanksgiving,'
'Honesty in Thanksgiving,'
'Uprightness in Thanksgiving,'
'Spontaneous Thanksgiving.'

Scripture

I Chronicles 29:1-19

Genesis 4:6-7; 12:2,7; 15:5; 17:4-8, 17; 22:1-2, 12; 37:5-11; 39:20

Exodus 35:5-7, 22; 36:6-7

Deuteronomy 8:11-20; 16:16-17

I Chronicles 17:1-14; 22:5, 7-10; 28:1-2, 11-19

Psalms 7:9-11; 11:4-7; 32:10-11; 37:34-40; 66:10; 97:10-11; 105:16-22

Proverbs 2:7-8, 20-22; 14:1

Malachi 1:7-8

II Corinthians 8:3-5; 9:6-8

Hebrews 11:17-18

James 1:12

Text: I Chronicles 29:17

A Few Versions of the Text, I Chronicles 29:17

I know also, my God, that You test the heart, and have pleasure in uprightness. As for me, in the uprightness of my heart I have willingly offered all these things; and now with joy I have seen Your people, who are present here, to offer willingly to You. *New King James Version*

I know also, my God, that thou triest the heart, and hast pleasure in uprightness. As for me, in the uprightness of my heart I have willingly offered all these things; and now have I seen with joy thy people that are present here, offer willingly unto thee. *The Wesleyan Bible Commentary*

I know, my God, that thou triest the heart, and hast pleasure in uprightness; in the uprightness of my heart I have freely offered all these things, and now I have seen thy people, who are present here, offering freely and joyously to thee. *Revised Standard Version*

I know, my God, that you test the heart, and are pleased with integrity. All these things have I given willingly and with honest intent. And now I have seen with joy how willingly your people who are here have given to you. *New International Version*

I know, O my God, that thou dost test the heart and that plain honesty pleases thee; with an honest heart I have given all these gifts willingly, and have rejoiced now to see thy people here present give willingly to thee. *The New English Bible Version*

I know, my God, that thou test men to see if they are good; for you enjoy good men. I have done all this with good motives, and I have watched your people offer their gifts willingly and joyously. *The Living Bible Illustrated*

I know, my God, that you examine hearts, and delight in honesty. With an honest heart I have willingly offered all these things. I've overjoyed to see your people here offering so willingly to you. *God's Word.*

Introduction

An elderly lady was ushered into the private office of the President Abraham Lincoln (February 12, 1809- April 15, 1865). He was the sixteenth President (March 1861- April 15,1865) of the U. S. A. The President asked the lady, "What can I do for you, Madam?" The lady placed a basket on the table and said to him, "Mr. President, I have come here today not to ask any favour for myself or for anyone. I heard that you were very fond of cookies and I came here to bring you this basket of cookies! " The President stood speechless for some time. Tears rolled on his cheeks and then he said, "My good woman, your thoughtful and unselfish deed greatly moves me. Thousands have come into this office since I became President, but you are the first one to come asking no favour for yourself or somebody else." [1] This event tells us that the President Abraham Lincoln was honest in giving thanks to the lady.

Charles Spurgeon (June 19, 1834- January 31, 1892) was a Baptist minister and a famous evangelist in England. Once his famous tabernacle had a pressing financial need. He called the board members for a meeting to pray for the solution of the problem. All members agreed that they need to pray until the Lord sent the supply. At this point Rev. Spurgeon interrupted and said, "Wait a minute! Before you begin this prayer meeting there is something I'd like to do." Taking a sheet of paper, he wrote, 'C. H. Spurgeon gives 50 pounds.' Then he passed it around others to write down how much they would give. When the subscriptions were totalled, the prayer meeting turned out to be a 'praise and glory' session, because the need had been fully met.[2] Rev. Spurgeon wanted to give to God's work as much as he could afford with honesty. His generous giving inspired others to do the same for the noble cause.

Introduction of the Text

The generous and sincere act of the Reverend Charles Spurgeon inspired his supporters to give generously and spontaneously to God's work. Their collective giving to God's work was the solution to their financial problem. When their problem was solved, they thanked God and praised Him. Church history is filled with such similar events. Israel, God's chosen people, often demonstrated the spirit of generosity whenever they were challenged to build or rebuild the temple for the LORD God.

King David (1002-962 B. C.) wished to thank the LORD God by building a temple for God. He made a blueprint of the temple; and presented his plan to his son, King Solomon (962-922 B. C.), with generous gifts from the royal treasury and his own treasury, in the presence of the leaders of Israel. Then he challenged the assembly saying, "Who will offer willingly, consecrating himself today to the LORD?" (I Chr. 29:5) Then all leaders gave gold, silver, bronze, iron, and precious stones for the proposed temple. Then all the people were inspired to contribute. They rejoiced when they gave willingly, whole heartedly and freely. King David and all the people rejoiced greatly. At this important event, King David said:

I know, my God, that thou triest the heart, and hast pleasure in uprightness; in the uprightness of my heart I have freely offered all these things, and now I have seen thy people, who are present here, offering freely and joyously to thee. (I Chr. 29:17)

This is the text of our meditation now.

The Context of the Text

The Lord God made David victorious over his enemies; He also made King David rich and prosperous. King David built a house of cedar for himself. While he was dwelling in the house, a thought came to him to build a house for the ark of the covenant of the LORD. He expressed this thought to prophet Nathan. Nathan said to David that God was with him; and he might do as he desired (I Chr. 17:1-2). The same night the LORD God spoke to Nathan and gave a message for King David, as follows:

Thus says the LORD: You shall not build me a house to dwell in. For I have not dwelt in a house since the day I led up Israel to this day, but I have gone from tent to tent and from dwelling to dwelling. In all places where I have moved with all Israel, did I speak a word with any of the judges of Israel, whom I commanded to shepherd my people, saying, "Why have you not built me a house of cedar?"... I took you from the pasture, from following the sheep, that you should be prince over my people Israel; and I have been with you wherever you went, and have cut off all your enemies from before you; and I will make for you a name, like the name of the great ones of the earth. And I will appoint a place for my people and will plant them, that they may dwell in their own place, and be disturbed no more... Moreover I declare to you that the LORD will build you a house. When your days are fulfilled to go to be with your fathers, I will raise up your offspring after you, one of your sons, and I will establish his kingdom. He shall build a house for me, and I will establish his throne for ever....I will confirm him in my house and in my kingdom for ever and his throne shall be established for ever. (I Chr. 17:4-14)

God did not allow King David to build a temple. When prophet Gad advised King David to build an altar on the threshing floor of Ornan, the Jebusite, David bought a piece of land from Ornan for six hundred shekels of gold (I Chr. 21:25) as the future site for the house of the LORD God and for the altar of burnt offering for Israel (I Chr. 22:1). Then King David went on collecting materials in great quantity for the house of the LORD God, before his death. He said to himself:

Solomon my son is young and inexperienced, and the house that is to be built for the LORD must be exceedingly magnificent, of fame and glory throughout all lands; I will therefore make preparation for it. (I Chr. 22:5)

Then King David charged King Solomon to build a house for the LORD, saying:

My son, I had it in my heart to build a house to the name of the LORD my God. But the word of the LORD came to me, saying, 'You have shed much blood and have waged great wars; you shall not build a house to my name, because you have shed so much blood before me upon the earth. Behold, a son shall be born to you; he shall be a man of peace... He shall build a house for my name. He shall be my son, and I will be his father, and I will establish his royal throne in Israel for ever. (I Chr. 22:7-10)

When King David was going to step down from the throne and hand over the kingdom to his son Solomon, he asked the leaders of the people to have a meeting with him. In that meeting, he offered his treasure to build a temple for God. Then he challenged the assembly saying, "Who will offer willingly, consecrating himself today to the LORD?" (I Chr. 29:5) Then all leaders gave gold, silver, bronze, iron, and precious stones for the proposed temple. Then all the people were inspired to contribute. They rejoiced when they gave willingly, whole heartedly, and freely. King David and all the people rejoiced greatly. At this important event, King David said:

> I know, my God, that thou triest the heart, and hast pleasure in uprightness; in the uprightness of my heart I have freely offered all these things, and now I have seen thy people, who are present here, offering freely and joyously to thee. (I Chr. 29:17)

This is the text of our mediation within its historical situation.

An Analysis of the Text

This text has four ideas. (A) The first idea is that King David knew that God tries heart of man.

(B) The second idea is that King David knew that God has pleasure in the uprightness of man.

(C) The third idea is that King David offered those things to build the house for the altar of the LORD God in his uprightness.

(D) The fourth idea is that King David saw the people of Israel offering things for God's house freely and joyously.

Exposition of the Ideas of the Text

(A) The first idea of the text is that King David knew that God tries heart of man. God tires the heart of man whether man will keep Him loving honestly and constantly or whether man will keep His commandments and the covenant when man will have everything in abundance.

King David knew that God tries heart of man from the scripture and from his own experience. God made a covenant with Abraham that God would make of him a great nation (Gen. 12:2). When Abraham was passing through the land of Canaan, God promised him to give the land to the descendants of Abraham (Gen. 12:7). While Abraham was childless, God promised him that his descendants would be innumerable (Gen. 15:5). When Abraham was ninety-nine years old, God made a covenant with Abraham that he would be a father of many nations and Canaan would be their promised land (Gen. 17:4-8). When Abraham was a hundred and Sarah, ninety, they had Isaac

(Gen. 17:17). God made Abraham very rich. Then God wanted to test whether Abraham would obey Him. God asked Abraham to offer Isaac, his only son, in sacrifice to Him (Gen. 22:1-2). Abraham was willing to do so. By his action in obedience to God, Abraham proved that he feared the LORD God (Gen. 22:12). Thus, God tested obedience of Abraham. Commenting on the event, the writer of the Letter to the Hebrews said:

> By faith Abraham, when he was tested, offered up Isaac, and he who had received the promises was ready to offer his only son, of whom it was said, "Through Isaac shall your descendants be named." He considered that God was able to raise men even from the dead; hence, figuratively speaking, he did receive him back. (Heb. 11:17-18)

God revealed His plan to Joseph through two dreams that He would make him a ruler that his brothers and parents would bow down before him (Gen. 37:5-11). Joseph told his dreams to his brothers and parents; and they were offended when they heard his dreams. Joseph had faith in God. In order to realize his dreams, Joseph had to go through slavery and imprisonment (Gen. 39:20). Through those difficult days, God was testing faith of Joseph. A psalm writer reflected on the life of Joseph in these words:

> When he summoned a famine on the land, and broke every staff of bread, he had sent a man ahead of them, Joseph, who was sold as a slave. His feet were hurt with fetters, his neck was put in a collar of iron; until what he had said came to pass the word of the LORD tested him. The king sent and released him, the ruler of the peoples set him free; he made him lord of his house, and ruler of all his possession, to instruct his princes at his pleasure, and to teach his elders wisdom. (Ps.105:16-22)

The people of Israel settled in Egypt, and they increased in number. But they were made slaves of Egyptians. They remained in slavery about four centuries (Gen. 15:13; Acts 7:6). God redeemed them from slavery through Moses. Moses led the people of Israel to the promised land through the wilderness. Before they entered the promised land, where they would have everything in abundance, Moses warned the people that they should not forget that the LORD God who gave them the promised land and He gave them everything. In his address, he said to the people of Israel:

> Take heed lest you forget the LORD your God, by not keeping his
> commandments and his ordinances, which I command you this day: lest,
> when you have eaten and are full, and have built goodly houses and live in
> them, and when your herds and flocks multiply, and your silver and gold is
> multiplied, and all that you have is multiplied, then your heart be lifted up,
> and you forget the LORD your God, who brought you out of the land of
> Egypt, out of the house of bondage, who led you through the great and
> terrible wilderness, with its fiery serpents and scorpions and thirsty ground
> where there was no water, who brought you water out of the flinty rock, who
> fed you in the wilderness with manna which your fathers did not know, that
> he might humble you and test you, to do you good in the end. Beware lest
> you say in your hear, 'My power and the might of my hand have gotten me
> this wealth.' You shall remember that the LORD your God, for it is he who
> gives you power to get wealth; that he may confirm his covenant which he
> swore to your fathers, as at this day. And if you forget the LORD your God
> and go after other gods and serve them and worship them, I solemnly warn
> you this day that you shall surely perish. Like the nations that the LORD
> makes to perish before you, so shall you perish, because you would not obey
> the voice of the LORD your God. (Deut. 8:11-20)

King David knew very well that the LORD God tests hearts of the
people; and rewards them accordingly. He expressed his conviction in
the following words:

> The LORD is in his holy temple, the LORD's throne is in heaven; his eyes
> behold, his eyelids test, the children of men. The LORD tests the righteous
> and the wicked, and his soul hates him that loves violence. On the wicked
> he will rain coals of fire and brimstone; a scorching will shall be the portion
> of their cup. For the LORD is righteous, he loves righteous deeds; the upright
> shall behold his face. (Ps. 11:4-7 cf. Ps. 7:9-11; Ps. 66:10)

The same conviction is repeated in the first part of the text of our
meditation now (I Chr. 29:17). St. James upheld the same conviction,
when he wrote to Christians these words:

> Blessed is the man who endures trial, for when he has stood the test he will
> receive the crown of life which God has promised to those who love him.
> (Jas. 1:12)

(B) The second idea of the text is that King David knew that God
has pleasure in the uprightness of man. God has delight in honesty
and integrity of man. He protects honest people; but He punishes

dishonest and wicked people. The LORD God is righteous; and honesty of man is an element of the total righteousness of man. King David expressed this conviction in the following words:

> Wait for the LORD, and keep to his way, and he will exalt you to possess the land; you will look on the destruction of the wicked. I have seen a wicked man overbearing, and towering like a cedar of Lebanon. Again I passed by, and, lo, he was no more; though I sought him, he could not be found. Mark the blameless man, and behold the upright, for there is posterity for the man of peace. But transgressors shall be altogether destroyed; the posterity of the wicked shall be cut off. The salvation of the righteous is from the LORD; he is their refuge in the time of trouble. The LORD helps them and delivers them; he delivers them from the wicked, and saves them, because they take refuge in him. (Ps. 37:34-40 cf. Ps. 7:10; 32:10-11; 97:10-12)

King Solomon, the writer of the Book of Proverbs, confirmed the conviction of King David, in various places, such as:

> So you will walk in the way of good men and keep to the paths of the righteous. For the upright will inhabit the land, and men of integrity will remain in it; but the wicked will be cut off from the land, and the treacherous will be rooted out of it. (Pr. 2:20-22; cf. Pr. 2:7-8; 14:11)

(C) The third idea of the text is that King David offered those things to build the house for the altar of the LORD God in his uprightness. God inspired King David to write down the details of the temple (I Chr. 28:19). King David wrote all the details of the proposed temple (I Chr. 28:11-18); and gave the master plan to his son Solomon. Then he called all the officials of Israel, mighty men, and officials (I Chr. 28:1-2). In their presence, he handed over the plan to King Solomon. Then he gave gold, silver, bronze, iron, coloured stones, marbles to build the things. He said to the assembly that he was giving those materials as far as he was able to give (I Chr. 29:2). Then from his personal treasury, he gave three thousand talents of gold, seven thousand talents of silver, and other materials (I Chr. 29:4-5). When he gave those materials, he told the assembly that he gave those things, because his devotion to the house of the LORD God (I Chr.29:3). King David demonstrated his honesty or integrity by giving so much for the house of God. King David expressed his gratitude to God by his generous offerings to the house of the LORD God. He gave to

God what was due to God. King David was doing what was commanded of God to the people of Israel, in the following words: "They shall not appear before the LORD empty-handed; every man shall give as he is able, according to the blessing of the LORD your God which he has given you." (Deut. 16:16-17)

It had been expected to serve the LORD God in offerings, according to the blessing of the LORD God. Adam had two sons: Cain and Abel. Cain was a farmer, and Abel, a shepherd. God blessed them in their business. In the course of time, Cain brought an offering of fruit of the ground, and his brother Abel brought an offering of the firstlings of his flock and of their fat portions. God had no regard to Cain and his offering; but God had regard for Abel and his offering. Abel's offering was made of the best of his things; but Cain's offering was not made of the best of his things. This was the reason why God approved Abel's offering and why God was not pleased with Cain's offering. Cain was very angry; and his countenance fell. Then God said to Cain:

> Why are you angry, and why has your countenance fallen? If you do well, will you not be accepted? And if you do not do well, sin is couching at the door; its desire is for you, but you must master it. (Gen. 4:6-7)

These words imply that dishonesty in giving to God is a kind of sin. There were many followers of Cain among Israel. They used to offer God defective animals in sacrifice. God was displeased with them. He said to those dishonest people through prophet Malachi:

> When you offer blind animals in sacrifice, is that no evil? And when you offer those that are lame or sick, is that no evil? Present that to your governor; will he be pleased with you or show you favour? says the LORD of hosts. And now entreat the favour of God, that he may be gracious to us. With such a gift from your hand, will he show favour to any of you? says the LORD of hosts. (Mal. 1:7-8)

In other words, God favours to those who are honest in their giving; and He expects people to serve Him in giving as He blesses them.

(D) The fourth idea of the text is that King David saw the people of Israel offering things for God's house freely and joyously. King David demonstrated his dedication to God's work by his generous offerings. Then he challenged the assembly, saying, "Who then will offer willingly, consecrating himself today to the LORD? " (I Chr. 29:5) The people took the challenge seriously; and they followed King David. They gave five thousand talents and ten thousand darics of gold, ten thousand talents of silver, eighteen thousand talents of bronze, and a hundred thousand talents of iron, and precious stones (I Chr. 29:7-8). Then all the people rejoiced, because they gave to God's work willingly and freely. King David also rejoiced greatly. Then King David blessed the LORD God, acknowledging that those things they received from the hand of God, in these words:

> But who am I, and what is my people, that we should be able thus to offer willingly? For all things come from thee, and of thy own have we given thee. ...O LORD our God, all this abundance that we have provided for building thee a house for thy holy name comes from thy hand and all is thy own. I know, my God, that thou triest the heart, and hast pleasure in uprightness; in the uprightness of my heart I have freely offered all these things, and now I have seen thy people, who are present here, offering freely and joyfully to thee. (I Chr. 29:14-17)

King David and the leaders of Israel were generous in their giving to the house of the LORD God. This event should remind us of a similar event when Moses presented a plan to build the tabernacle for God. He called the people together and said:

> Take from among you an offering to the LORD; whoever is of a generous heart, let him bring the LORD's offering: gold, silver, bronze, linen, skins of goat and of rams, wood, and stone. (Ex. 35:5-7)

Then people left Moses and they returned; everyone whose heart stirred him, and everyone whose spirit moved him, and brought offerings to build the tabernacle for the LORD God. They presented their offerings with willing hearts (Ex. 35:22). Their offerings were more than required; therefore, the people were restrained from bringing the offerings to the LORD (Ex. 36:6-7). Moses issued such an order.

The spirit of generous giving to God's work was adopted by Christians of the early Church. The churches in Macedonia were liberal in their giving. St. Paul wrote about this, in these words:

> For they gave according to their means, and beyond their means, of their own free will, begging us earnestly for the favour of taking part in the relief of the saints - and this, not as we expected, but first they gave themselves to the Lord and to us by the will of God. (II Cor. 8:3-5)

St. Paul exhorted the Corinthians to be generous in their giving to the work of God, in these words:

> The point is this: he who sows sparingly will also reap sparingly, and he who sows bountifully will also reap bountifully. Each one must do as he has made up his mind, not reluctantly or under compulsion, for God loves a cheerful giver. And God is able to provide you with every blessing in abundance so that you may always have enough of everything and may provide in abundance for every good work. (II Cor. 9:6-8)

Conclusion

God blesses people abundantly; and He tests whether they would be honest in acknowledging Him that He blessed them abundantly. God also has delight in honesty and integrity of man, when man gives his tithes of every thing and freewill offerings to His work. The freewill offering to God's work causes people to be joyous; and the event turns into a joyful thanksgiving.

The thanksgiving service should make us to reflect on the variety of questions, such as: Are our hearts right with God? Are we serving God by offering to Him in the proportion that He blessed us? Are we honest and integrated in giving to God's work? Do we generously and joyfully give our time, and talents to God's work?

Let us be thankful to God for all His blessings; and subsequently serve Him in giving our tithes and freewill offerings joyfully and spontaneously.

Recommended Hymns from the Methodist Hymnal

524   'My God, I thank Thee, who hast made'

851   'All things bright and beautiful,'

968   'Yes, God is good - in earth and sky,'

969   'O Lord of heaven and earth and sea,'

Recommended Responsive Reading from the Methodist Hymnal

61 (p. 411)

Recommended Responsive Reading from *A Worship Manual for Scriptural or Methodist Order of Service*

59 (pp. 161-163).

Endnotes

[1] Paul Lee Tan, Encyclopedia of 7700 Illustrations: Signs of the Time, (Rockville, Maryland: Assurance Publishers, 9th Printing, 1985) # 4547.

[2] *Ibid.,* # 4671.

Chapter 4

Titles of the Sermon
'Thanksgiving Services,'
'Honouring God by Thanksgiving,'
'Ordering Aright by Thanksgiving,'
'Thanksgiving Linked with Salvation.'

Scripture
Psalms 50:7-23
Genesis 4:2-7; 14:1-20; 22:1-14
II Kings 18:13-19:37; 20:1-11
I Chronicles 16:8-13, 23-25, 35-36; 17:1-15; 28:1-7, 11-19;
29:1-15
II Chronicles 29:5-11; 38:24
Nehemiah 13:10-13
Psalms 37:39; 62:2; 107:17-22
Proverbs 3:9-10
Isaiah 12:2; 25:9
Malachi 3:7-12

Text: Psalms 50:23

A Few Versions of the Text, Psalms 50:23
Whoever offers praise glorifies Me; and to him who orders his conduct aright I will show the salvation of God. *The New King James Version*

Whoso offereth the sacrifice of thanksgiving glorifieth me; And to him that ordereth his way aright Will I show the salvation of God. *The Wesleyan Bible Commentary*

He who brings thanksgiving as his sacrifice honours me; to him who orders his way aright I will show the salvation of God. *Revised Standard Version*

He who sacrifices thanks offerings honors me, and he prepares the way so that I may show him the salvation of God. *New International Version*

He who offers a sacrifice of thanksgiving does me due honour, and to him who follows my way I will show the salvation of God. *The New English Bible*

But true praise is a worthy sacrifice; this really honors me. Those who walk my paths will receive salvation from the Lord. *The Living Bible Illustrated*

Whoever offers thanks as a sacrifice honors me. I will let everyone who continues in my way see the salvation that comes from God. *God's Word*

Introduction

Thanksgiving Sunday service had been annually conducted in every Christian congregation or church; the practice to hold thanksgiving service every year has become universal. Some countries, like Canada and the U. S. A., have developed their secular traditions to justify thanksgiving service. Thanksgiving service is a most important service in the life of Church.

Introduction of the Text

The Bible contains some events, when the people of God thanked God, and how they thanked Him. The religious practice of thanking God for His blessings has been theologically justified by the utterances of the LORD God. One of those divine sayings is as follows:

He who brings thanksgiving as his sacrifice honours me; to him who orders his way aright I will show the salvation of God. (Ps. 50:23)

This is the text of our meditation now.

An Analysis of the Text

This text has three ideas. (A) The first idea is that a person, who brings thanksgiving as his or her sacrifice, honours God.

(B) The second idea is that the person, who brings thanksgiving sacrifice, shows that he or she has ordered his or her life aright in the sight of God.

(C) The third idea is that God will show him or her His salvation.

Exposition of the Ideas of the Text

(A) The first idea of the text is that a person, who brings thanksgiving as his or her sacrifice, honours God. In other words, there are other ways to honour God; but to bring thanksgiving sacrifice to God is a most significant and honest way to praise God among various ways of honouring God. This is a concrete way of expressing inner feelings of gratitude to God; this is a very visible way to say thanks to the LORD God for His blessings.

The way of honouring God by thanksgiving sacrifice was established from antiquity. There are some events in the Bible to emphasize the idea.

(1) Adam and Eve, the first human couple, had two sons - Abel and Cain. They were blessed by God in their works. They brought thanksgiving sacrifice to thank God. God was pleased with Abel's thanksgiving sacrifice, because Abel gave to God what was a best portion of his possession. On the other hand, God was not pleased with Cain's thanksgiving sacrifice, because it was not a best portion of his possession. (Gen. 4:2-7)

(2) Ched-or-laomer, the king of Elam, was ruling over five kingdoms- of Sodom, Gamorrah, Admah, Zebolim, and Bela- for twelve years. The five kings of those kingdoms revolted against the king of

Elam in the thirteenth year. In order to re-establish a control over them, the king of Elam asked the kings of other four kingdoms - of Shinar, Ellasar, Golim, and Eliasar- to crush down the revolt. The forces of those kingdoms were fighting in the Valley of Siddim (i. e. Salt Sea). The king of Elam and his fellow kings defeated other kings; and they took all the goods of Sodom and Gomorrah, and Lot, a nephew of Abram, and his possession.

Abram learned about the tragic capture of his nephew. He asked his allies- Eshcol and Aner- to fight against the king of Elam and his allies. Abram was successful in defeating the kings; and he brought back all goods and the captured people.

The king of Sodom went to meet Abram at the Valley of Shaveh; Melchizedek, the king of Salem, also went to meet Abram in order to appreciate his victory over their enemies. Melchizedek was not only a king; but he was also a priest of God Most High. Melchizedek blessed Abram in the name of God Most High. Abram gave Melchizedek a tenth of everything, which he got in his victory. (Gen. 14:1-20) This is how the practice of honouring God with tithes of everything came into being. This religious practice originated with Abram.

Abram loved the LORD God so much that he was willing to sacrifice his only son Isaac to God, when God wanted to test faith of Abram (Gen. 22:1-14). Abram obeyed the voice of God always. He was always ready and willing to give everything to God as his thanksgiving sacrifice.

(3) When King David (1002-962 B. C.) brought up the ark of covenant from the house of Obededam to Jerusalem and kept it inside the tent, he offered to God burnt offerings and peace offerings. He blessed the people in the name of the LORD God; and he gave them food.

Then King David appointed Levites as ministers to praise God and to thank Him. He appointed Asaph and his brothers to sing thanksgiving hymns or psalms to the LORD. King David sang a psalm of thanksgiving to God. The following are the selected verses from that psalm:

> O give thanks to the LORD, call on his name, make known his deed among the peoples! Sing to him, sing praises to him, tell of all his wonderful works! Glory in his holy name; let the hearts of those who seek the LORD rejoice! See the LORD and his strength, seek his presence continually! Remember the wonderful works that he has done, the wonders he wrought, the judgments he uttered, O offspring of Abraham his servant, sons of Jacob, his chosen ones! (I Chr. 16:8-13)

> Sing to the LORD, all the earth! Tell of his salvation from day to day. Declare his glory among the nations, his marvellous works among all the peoples! For great is the LORD, and greatly to be praised, and he is to be held in awe above all gods. (I Chr. 16:23-25)

> Deliver us, O God of our salvation, and gather and save us from among the nations, that we may give thanks to thy holy name, and glory in thy praise. Blessed be the LORD, the God of Israel from everlasting to everlasting! (I Chr. 16:35-36)

(4) King David built a palace for his family and occupied it. He was thinking of building a temple for the LORD God. He spoke about his intention to prophet Nathan. Nathan gave his consent to David, because God was with David. Then Nathan received the word of God for King David. Nathan told King David that God did not permit him to build the temple, because he shed much blood; but his son would build a temple for God (I Chr. 17:1-15). After a few years, King David called the officials of Israel and told them that he had a plan to build a house for the ark of covenant of the LORD. He made preparation for building; but God told him that his son Solomon would build the house of God (I Chr. 28:1-7). Then King David submitted his plan of the temple to his son, King Solomon (962-922 B. C.) and provided gold, silver, stone, wood, and other things (I Chr. 28:11-19; 29:1-15). He also gave similar things from his own treasury. King David did so much, because he thanked God for making him a king from an ordinary family, and for many divine blessings.

King David challenged other leaders to offer freewill offerings; and all of them gave willingly. They all rejoiced in giving to God's work (I Chr. 29:6-9).

(5) King Solomon (962-922 B. C.) continued the practice of liberal giving to God's work. He exhorted the people of God to honour God with liberal giving, in the following words:

> Honor the LORD with your substance and with the first fruit of all your produce, then your barns will be filled with plenty, and your vats will be bursting with wine. (Pr. 3:9-10)

(B) The second idea of the text is that the person, who brings thanksgiving sacrifice, shows that he or she has ordered his or her life aright in the sight of God. In other words, a person, who honours God with tithes of everything and freewill offerings, walks right with God; he or she is a righteous person. On the other hand, a person, who does not honour God with tithes of everything and freewill offerings, is not a righteous person, because he or she does not obey God's commandment, and is not right with God. God rewards the righteous and punishes the wicked. There are some examples to illustrate the idea.

(1) King Hezekiah (715-687 B. C.), a king of Judah, took notice of how the people turned away from God's commandment, and why God punished them for the neglect of their religious duties and practices. He addressed the people of Judah, in the following words:

> Hear me, Levites! Now sanctify yourselves, and sanctify the house of the LORD, the God of your fathers, and carry out the filth from the holy place. For our fathers have been unfaithful and have done what was evil in the sight of the LORD our God; they have forsaken him, and have turned away their faces from the habitation of the LORD, and turned their backs. They also shut the doors of the vestibule and put out the lamps, and have not burned incense or offered burnt offerings in the holy place to the God of Israel. Therefore the wrath of the LORD came on Judah and Jerusalem, and he has made them an object of horror, of astonishment, and of hissing, as you see with your own eyes. For lo, our fathers have fallen by the sword and our sons and our daughters and our wives are in captivity for this. Now it is in my heart to make a covenant with the LORD, the God of Israel, that his fierce

anger may turn away from us. My sons, do not be negligent, for the LORD
has chosen you to stand in his presence, to minister to him, and to be his
ministers and burn incense to him. (II Chr. 29:5-11)

In this passage, neglect of religious duties includes honouring God
with tithes of everything and freewill offerings. As the people of Israel
neglected their religious duties, God was angry with them; and He
punished them by sending them into captivity. King Hezekiah realized
this fact; and he subsequently appealed the people of Judah to turn
to the LORD God and to minister Him.

(2) The Levites were the priests, serving God in the temple. They
were given a portion from the tithes of everything for their services.
When the people of Israel neglected attending the temple of God,
it had affected some Levites to give up their temple duties.
Nehemiah, the governor of Judah (445-433 B. C.) found that the
Levites were not given their portion; therefore, they stopped their
work in the temple; and they went to work on their fields. Nehemiah
remonstrated the officials and ordered them to bring tithes; and
he thus restored the order in the house of God (Neh. 13:10-13).

(3) God spoke through prophet Malachi about the seriousness of
honouring God with the tithes of everything. He said:

From the days of your fathers you have turned aside from my statutes and
have not kept them. Return to me, and I will return to you, says the LORD
of host. But you say, 'How shall we return?' Will man rob God? You are
robbing me. But you say, 'How are we robbing thee? In your tithes and
offerings. You are cursed with a curse, for you are robbing me; the whole
nation of you. Bring the full tithes into the storehouse, that there may be
food in my house; and thereby put me to the test, says the LORD of host,
if I will not open the windows of heaven for you and pour down for you
an overflowing blessing. I will rebuke the devourer for you, so that it will
not destroy the fruits of your soil; and your wine in the field shall not fail
to bear, says the LORD of hosts. Then all nations will call you blessed, for
you will be a land of delight, says the LORD of hosts. (Mal. 3:7-12)

In these words, God asked the people of Israel to honour Him with
their tithes. He would bless them with abundance, if they obey His
command to serve Him with tithes of everything.

(C) The third idea of the text is that God will show him or her His salvation. In other words, God will show His salvation to the person, who honours Him with the tithes of everything and freewill offerings, and who walks aright with God. What did the psalm writer mean 'the salvation of God?' He described the salvation of God as conditional in the following words:

> Offer to God a sacrifice of thanksgiving, and pay your vows to the Most High; and call upon me in the day of trouble; I will deliver you, and you shall glorify me. (Ps. 50:14-15)

A similar thought is expressed by another psalm writer, defining salvation of God.

Some were sick through their sinful ways, and because of their iniquities suffered affliction; they loathed any kind of food and they drew near to the gates of death. They cried to the LORD in their trouble, and He delivered them from their distress; He sent forth His word, and He healed them, and delivered them from destruction. Let them thank the LORD for His steadfast love, for His wonderful works to the sons of men! And let them offer sacrifices of thanksgiving, and tell of His deeds in songs of joy! (Ps. 107:17-22)

Herein salvation means that God heals people from bodily sickness; and He delivers them from distress and destruction. Other writers confirmed the idea saying, God becomes the refuge for the righteous in the time of their troubles (Ps. 37:39; 62:2; Is. 12:2; 25:9). This thought is illustrated by some events.

(1) When King Hezekiah (715-687 B. C.) was very sick and at the point of death, he prayed to the LORD (II Chr. 32:24). God heard the prayer of King Hezekiah; He healed him, and He added fifteen years to the life of King Hezekiah. (II Kg. 20:1-11).

(2) When Sennacherib, the king of Assyria (705-681 B. C.), besieged Jerusalem in ca. 701 B. C., King Hezekiah (715-687 B. C.) and the people of Jerusalem cried to the LORD, and God delivered them from destruction (II Kg. 18:13-19:37).

Conclusion

The LORD God provided the people in abundance. He expected His people to acknowledge that those blessings were from Him. Subsequently God expected His people to honour Him with the tithes of everything. He commanded them to worship Him with thanksgiving sacrifices and freewill offerings. He made His blessings conditional. He blessed those who obeyed His commandments; and He punished those who disobeyed Him. He delivered His faithful and obedient servants from troubles and destruction. God is ever faithful in keeping His covenant and promises; and He expects of man to thank Him sincerely in terms of giving tithes and freewill offerings to Him.

Recommended Hymns from the Methodist Hymnal

8   'O worship the King,'

550   'O For a heart to praise my God,'

851   'All things bright and beautiful,'

968   'Yes, God is good- in earth and sky,'

Recommended Responsive Reading from the Methodist Hymnal

61 (p. 411)

Recommended Responsive Reading from *A Worship Manual for Scriptural or Methodist Order of Service*

59 (pp. 161-163).

Chapter 5

Titles of the Sermon
'Recalling Divine Benefits,'
'Forgetting Divine Benefits,'
'All-inclusive Gratitude.'

Scripture
Psalms 103:1-22

Exodus 20:4-6

Deuteronomy 5:8-10; 6:10-15; 7:9-16; 8:11-20; 28:58-61

Joshua 24:13-14

II Samuel 11:2-5, 15-25; 12:9-13

Nehemiah 1:8-11

Ezra 3:10-13

Psalms 28:6-7; 37:25; 38:1-8; 40:1-4; 41:1-3; 51:1-4,11-14; 88:3-7

Isaiah 38:1-6

Daniel 3:13-26; 6:16-23; 9:3-19

Matthew 4:23-25; 6:31-33; 9:35; 10:1

Luke 17:11-15

Ephesians 2:4-7

Text: Psalms 103:2-5

A Few Versions of the Text, Psalms 103:2-5

Bless the LORD, O my soul; And forget not all His benefits: Who forgives all your iniquities, Who heals all your diseases, Who redeems your life from destruction, Who crowns you with loving kindness and tender mercies, Who satisfies your mouth with good things, So that your youth is renewed like the eagle's. *New King James Version*

Bless Jehovah, O my soul; And forget not all his benefits: Who forgiveth all thine iniquities; Who healeth all your diseases; Who redeemeth thy life from destruction; Who crowneth thee with loving kindness and tender mercies; Who satisfies thy desire with good things, So that thy youth is renewed like the eagle. *The Wesleyan Bible Commentary*

Bless the LORD, O my soul, and forget not all his benefit, who forgives all your iniquity, who heals all your diseases, who redeems your life from the Pit, who crowns you with steadfast love and mercy, who satisfies you with good as long as you live, so that your youth is renewed like the eagle's. *Revised Standard Version*

Praise the LORD, O my soul, and forget not all his benefits. He forgives all your sins and heals all your diseases; he redeems my life from pit and crowns me with love and compassion. He satisfies my desires with good things, so that my youth is renewed like the eagle's. *New International Version*

Bless the LORD, O my soul, and forget none of his benefits. He pardons all my guilt and heals all my suffering. He rescues me from the pit of death and surrounds me with constant love, and tender affection; he contents me with good in the prime of life, and my youth is ever new like an eagle's. *The New English Bible*

Yes, I will bless the Lord and not forget the glorious things he does for me. He forgives all my sins. He heals me. He ransoms me from hell. He surrounds me with loving kindness and tender mercies. He fills my life with good things! My youth is renewed like the eagle's! *The Living Bible Illustrated*

Praise the LORD, my soul, and never forget all the good he has done: He is the one who forgives all your sins, the one who heals all your diseases, the one who rescues your life from the pit, the one who crowns you with mercy and compassion, the one who fills your life with blessings so that you become young again like an eagle. *God's Word*

Introduction

(1) It is a human tendency to ask God for His blessings always, but to thank God rarely for those blessings, which He bestows upon the needy persons. This tendency is reflected through a legend as follows.

Once God decided to send two angels on earth to gather up prayers of people and also to gather up thanksgiving of the people. God gave them a basket each. One angel was assigned to gather up the petition of the people and another angel, to gather up prayers of thanksgiving. Those two angels travelled the whole earth; and they went back to heaven to deliver those baskets to God. One baskets had heaped high, and running over, with innumerable petitions of the people. Another basket was almost empty. The angel, who was carrying the basket of prayers of thanksgiving, had searched the earth very diligently but his basket remained almost empty. [1]

This legend tells us that the people forget to thank God, whenever God answers their petitions; and they keep on asking for more and more. A right thing for us to do is to remember to thank God for His blessings and benefits.

(2) During Christmas season, many children write to Santa Claus for various kinds of gifts. Santa Claus replies every letter. From the letters of Santa Claus, parents of the children get clues as to what their children expect to receive as Christmas gifts; and they buy those gifts. After Christmas, Santa Claus hardly receives a letter of thank from the children; they forget to thank Santa Claus. [2]

(3) Britain, Canada, the U. S. A., and other developed nations have developed social welfare system. When a person becomes unemployed, he or she is given an unemployment benefit. When a person is handicapped and therefore unemployable, he or she is

given social welfare beneits, including free medical prescriptions. The U. S. A. governmentment gives food stamps to the people, who are on the social welfare. It is expected of the people, who receive these benefits, to be thankful to their government; but the recipients are not thankful for the benefits.

A hippie couple was planning their day by co-ordinating their activities. One of the couple said to the other, "I am going over and pick up my unemployment cheque. Then I'll drop in the university to see what's holding up my cheque for my federal education grant. After that I'll pick up our food stamps. Meanwhile, you go over to the free clinic and check your tests, pick up my new glasses at the health centre, then go to the Welfare Department and apply for an increase in our eligibility limit. Then I'll meet you at 5 O'clock at the Federal Building for the mass demonstration against the rotten establishment." [3]

This is how majority of the people on the social welfare reacts towards their Social Welfare System. They lack a sense of being grateful to the government. On the contrary, they become excessively critical of the establishment and revolt against it, calling it a rotten system.

(4) There is a wide-spread tendency among the people not to thank the person, who does them some good; and they do not give thanks to God for His divine good acts. This idea is evident in an event or the miracle, performed by Jesus Christ, as follows.

Jesus Christ entered a village, situated between Samaria and Galilee, on His way to Jerusalem. Ten lepers met Jesus Christ; and they cried to him saying, "Jesus, Master, have mercy on us." Jesus Christ said to them, "go and show yourselves to the priests." One of them saw that he was healed on his way to the priests. He turned back and went to see Jesus Christ. He fell on his face at the feet of Jesus Christ, giving Him thanks. The leper, who gave thanks to Jesus Christ was a Samaritan, a foreigner. Then Jesus Christ asked the people, who were around him, "Were not ten cleansed? Where are the nine? Was no one found to return and give praise to God except this foreigner? (Lk. 17:11-15) The other nine were Jews, who were cured of leprosy, but they forgot to give thanks to Jesus Christ.

Introduction of the Text

To give thanks to others for the help they give in the time of need, to appreciate the government for the welfare benefit, and to thank God for His blessings- these are the right things to do. Specially giving thanks to God for the numerous blessing is the teaching of the Bible, the word of God. King David, who wrote many psalms, instructed himself to give thanks to God, in these words:

> **Bless the LORD, O my soul, and forget not all his benefits, who forgives all your iniquity, who heals all your diseases, who redeems your life from the Pit, who crowns you with steadfast love and mercy, who satisfies you with good as long as you live- so that your youth is renewed like the eagles.** (Psalms 103:2-5)

This is the text of our meditation.

An Analysis of the Text

In this text, King David exhorted himself to bless the LORD God or to give thanks to God for various blessings, which he received from God. This text has a number of ideas.

(A) The first idea is not to forget all divine benefits.

(B) The second idea is to remember and to thank God, because He forgives all sins or iniquity of man.

(C) The third idea is to thank God, because He heals all diseases.

(D) The fourth idea is to thank God, because He redeems man's life from the Pit.

(E) The fifth ideas is to thank God, because He crowns man with steadfast love and mercy.

(F) The sixth idea is to thank God, because He satisfies man with good things as long as he lives.

(G) The seventh idea is a result of the divine providence, which is that man's youth is renewed like eagles.

Exposition of the Ideas of the Text

(A) The first idea of the text is not to forget all divine benefits. One of the illustrations in the introduction told us that the nine lepers, who were healed by Jesus Christ, did not go back to Him to thank Him or to thank God for God's miraculous healing; but they forgot to thank God and to praise Him. There is a human tendency to forget benefactors, including God.

When Rev. Dr. Dwight Layman Moody (February 5, 1837-December 22,1899), a well known Methodist evangelist of the past, was reading Psalm 103: 2, "Bless the LORD, O my soul, and forget not all his benefit," he stopped at the verse; and said, "You can not remember 'em all, of course, but don't forget 'em all. Remember some of them."[4]

It is a human tendency to forget God, who is the source of all benefits, when man is happy and is enjoying material prosperity. Moses warned the people of Israel against this particular tendency, before they entered the promised land. He said to them:

> And when the LORD your God brings you into the land which he swore to your fathers, to Abraham, to Isaac, and to Jacob, to give you, with great and goodly cities, which you did not build, and houses full of good things, which you did not fill, and cisterns hewn out, which you did not hew, and vineyards and olive trees, which you did not plant, and when you eat and are full, then take heed lest you forget the LORD, who brought you out of the land of Egypt, out of the house of bondage. You shall fear the LORD your God; you shall serve him, and swear by his name. You shall not go after other gods, of the gods of the people who are round about you; for the LORD your God in the midst of you is a jealous God; lest the anger of the LORD your God be kindled against you, and he destroy you from off the face of the earth. (Deut. 6:10-15)

Moses repeated the solemn waring on another occasion, when he said:

> Take heed lest you forget the LORD your God, by not keeping his commandments and his ordinances and his statutes, which I command you this day; lest, when you have eaten and are full and have built goodly houses and live in them, and when your herds and flock multiply, and your silver and gold is multiplied, then your heart be lifted up, and you forget the LORD your God, who brought you out of the land of Egypt, out of the house

of bondage, who led you through the great and terrible wilderness, with its fiery serpents and scorpions and thirsty ground where there was no water, who brought you water out of the flinty rock, who fed you in the wilderness with manna which your fathers did not know, that he might humble you and test you, to do you good in the end. Beware lest you in your heart say, 'My power and the might of my hand have gotten me this wealth.' You shall remember the LORD your God, for it is he who gives you power to get wealth; that he may confirm his covenant which he swore to your fathers, as at this day. And if you forget the LORD your God and go after other gods and serve them and worship them, I solemnly warn you this day that you shall surely perish. Like the nations that the LORD makes to perish before you, so shall you perish, because you would not obey the voice of the LORD your God. (Deut. 8:11-20)

(B) The second idea is to remember and to thank God, because He forgives all sins or iniquity of man. King David (1002-962 B. C.) said this out of his own personal experience. King David committed an adultery with Bathsheba, the wife of his faithful soldier named Uriah the Hittite (II Sam. 11:2-5), and who was treacherously killed on the battle field (II Sam. 11:15-25). After this God sent prophet Nathan to King David to deliver His judgment in the following words:

Why have you despised the word of the LORD, to do what is evil in his sight? You have smitten Uriah the Hittite with the sword, and have taken his wife to be your wife, and have slain him with the sword of the Ammonites. Now therefore the sword shall never depart from your house, because you have despised me, and have taken the wife of Uriah the Hittite to be your wife. Thus says the LORD, 'Behold, I will raise up evil against you out of your house; and I will take your wives before your eyes, and give them to your neighbour, and he shall lie with your wives in the sight of this sun. For you did it secretly; but I will do this thing before all Israel and before the sun. (II Sam. 12:9-12)

When King David heard God's judgment, he said to prophet Nathan, confessing, "I have sinned against the LORD." (II Sam. 12: 13) As King David truly repented of his sin, prophet Nathan said to King David, "The LORD also has put away your sin; you shall not die." (II Sam. 12:13)

This event made King David to compose the psalm number 51. Let us quote a few verses from the psalm to confirm the point:

> Have mercy on me, O God, according to thy steadfast love; according to thy abundant mercy blot out my transgressions. Wash me thoroughly from my iniquity, and cleanse me from my sin! For I know my transgressions, and my sin is ever before me. Against thee, thee only, have I sinned, and done that which is evil in thy sight, so that thou art justified in thy sentence and blameless in thy judgement (Ps. 51:1-4)

After these verses, King David added:

> Cast me not away from thy presence, and take not thy holy Spirit from me. Restore to me the joy of thy salvation, and uphold me with a willing spirit. Then I will teach transgressors thy ways, and sinners will return to thee. Deliver me from blood-guiltiness, O God, thou God of my salvation, and my tongue will sing aloud of thy deliverance. (Ps. 51:11-14)

King David promised herein to praise God, because God granted him forgiveness of his sin. He remembered how God forgave his iniquity and gave him the joy of salvation.

(C) The third idea is to thank God, because He heals all diseases. King David exhorted the people of Israel to thank God, because He heals all diseases. We do not know whether King David suffered from any serious disease. But he expressed the biblical faith that God causes man to suffer for his sin, when he wrote:

> O LORD, rebuke me not in thy anger, nor chasten me in thy wrath! For thy arrows have sunk into me, and thy hand has come down on me. There is no soundness in my flesh because of thy indignation; there is no health in my bones because of my sin. For my iniquities have gone over my head; they weigh like a burden too heavy for me. My wounds grow foul and fester because of my foolishness, I am utterly bowed down and prostrate; all the day I go about mourning. For my loins are filled with burning, and there is no soundness in my flesh. I am utterly spent and crushed; I groan because of the tumult of my heart. (Ps. 38: 1-8)

King David's religious conviction about sin and sufferings seems to be based on the word of God, as follows:

> If you are not careful to do all the words of this law which are written in this book, that you may fear this glorious and awful name, the LORD your God, then the LORD will bring on you and your offspring extraordinary affliction, affliction severe and lasting, and sickness grievous and lasting. And he will bring upon you again all the diseases of Egypt, which you were afraid of; and they shall cleave to you. Every sickness also, and every affliction which

is not recorded in the book of this law, the LORD will bring upon you, until you are destroyed. (Deut. 28:58-61)

When man humbles himself and ask for God's mercy, God heals him. King David expressed this faith in another psalm:

The LORD delivers him in the day of trouble; the LORD protects him and keeps him alive; he is called blessed in the land; thou dost not give him up to the will of his enemies. The LORD sustains him on his sickbed; in his illness thou healest all his infirmities. (Ps. 41:1-3)

There are a few examples of how God heard cries of persons and healed their diseases. King Hezekiah (715-687 B. C.) became sick and was at the point of death. Prophet Isaiah went to see the King Hezekiah with the message of God: "Set your house in order; for you shall die, you shall not recover." (Is. 38:1) Then King Hezekiah prayed to God and wept bitterly. Then God sent prophet Isaiah back to the king with the message: "I have heard your prayer, I have seen your tears; behold, I will add fifteen years to your life." (Is. 38:5) God healed King Hezekiah from severe sickness..

The healing power of God was manifested through the healing miracles of Jesus Christ. It is recorded that Jesus Christ healed every disease and infirmity among the people in Galilee, Syria, Judea and beyond the Jordan (Mt. 4:23-25; 9:35). Jesus Christ gave the same power of healing to His twelve disciples (Mt. 10:1). God's healing ministry continues through the believers even now.

When God grants healing to those, who believe in His power and the Name, they should praise God and thank Him. It is expected of them.

(D) The fourth idea is to thank God, because He redeems man's life from the Pit. King David, in another psalm, thanked God, because God redeemed his life from the Pit, as follows:

I waited patiently for the LORD; he inclined to me and heard my cry. He drew me up from the desolate pit, out of the miry bog, and set my feet upon a rock, making my steps secure. He put a new song in my mouth, a song of praise to our God. Many will see and fear, and put their trust in the LORD. (Ps. 40:1-4)

The Pit is also called Sheol. Another psalm writer described the Sheol as the place of forgetfulness and the place of punishment, in the following verses:

> For my soul is full of troubles, and my life draws near to Sheol. I am reckoned among those who go down to the Pit; I am a man who has no strength, like one forsaken among the dead, like the slain that lie in the grave, like those whom thou dost remember no more, for they are cut off from thy hand. Thou hast put me in the depths of the Pit, in the regions dark and deep. Thy wrath lies heavy upon me, and thou dost overwhelm me with all thy waves. (Ps. 88:3-7)

The Pit or Sheol symbolizes deep trouble for man. When man cries for God to redeem or relieve from his troubles, God responds to the cry. This has been experience of many devout people. King David thanked God, when God redeemed him from his deep sorrows, in these words:

> Blessed is the LORD! For he has heard the voice of my supplication. The LORD is my strength and my shield; in him my heart trusts; so I am helped, and my heart exults, and with my song I give thanks to him. (Ps. 28:6-7)

There are many examples to confirm this point that God redeemed His servants from all deep troubles, even from life-threatening conditions. Shadrach, Meshach, and Abednego were kept safe and unharmed in the fiery furnace (Dan. 3:13-26). Daniel was kept safe and unharmed in lions' den (Dan. 6:16-23). God protected and defended the city of Jerusalem from the attack of Assyria, when king Hezekiah, the king of Judah, prayed to the LORD God (Is. 38:2-6).

(E) The fifth ideas is to thank God, because He crowns man with steadfast love and mercy. God has made His covenants and promises conditional, expecting the people to keep His commandments and statutes. He spoke to the people of Israel several times about the conditionality of His covenants, for example:

> You shall not make for yourself a graven image, or any likeness of anything that is in heaven above, or that is in the earth beneath, or that is in the water under the earth; you shall not bow down to them or serve them; for I the LORD your God is a jealous God, visiting the iniquity of the fathers upon the children to the third and the fourth generation of those who hate me,

but showing steadfast love to thousands of those who love me and keep my commandments. (Ex. 20:4-6; Deut. 5:8-10)

In other words, God would punish the people if they disobey His commandments; and He would maintain His love to those who would keep His commandments. This is how God made His love towards the people of Israel conditional.

The conditionality of the divine love had been reiterated by Moses, the servant God, who was inspired to write the laws of God for the people of Israel. He said to them:

> Know therefore that the LORD your God is God, the faithful God who keeps covenant and steadfast love with those who love him and keep his commandments, to a thousand generations, and requites to their face those who hate him, by destroying them; he will not be slack with him who hates him, he will requite him to his face. You shall therefore be careful to do the commandment, and the statutes, and the ordinances, which I command you this day. (Deut. 7:9-11 cf. Deut. 7:12-16)

Nehemiah, in the exile, became a cupbearer of King Artaxerxes I (465-424 B. C) (Neh. 2:1); he became concerned for the well-being of the city of Jerusalem. He prayed to the LORD God to look graciously upon the city of Jerusalem, confessing sins of his people, as follows:

> Remember the word which thou didst command thy servant Moses, saying, 'If you are unfaithful, I will scatter you among the peoples; but if you return to me and keep my commandments and do them, though your disperse be under the farthest skies, I will gather them thence and bring them to the place which I have chosen, to make my name dwell there' ... O LORD, let thy ear be attentive to the prayer of thy servant, to the prayer of thy servants who delight to fear thy name; and give success to thy servant today, and grant him mercy in the sight of this man. (Neh. 1:8-11)

In a similar way Daniel, while in the exile, prayed for the city of Jerusalem and asked God for forgiveness and mercy (Dan. 9:3-19).

God forgave the sins of His people; and He showed His steadfast love and mercy to them, and redeemed them from the captivity, and enabled them to build the city of Jerusalem and the temple. He made them free once again. They thanked God for His mercy and love (Ezra 3:10-13)

That steadfast love and mercy has been shown to Christians by God in Jesus Christ. St. Paul wrote to the Ephesians about this, in these words:

> But God, who is rich in mercy, out of the great love with which he loved us, even when we were dead through our trespasses, made us alive together with Christ (by grace you have been saved), and raised us up with him, and made us sit with him in the heavenly places in Christ Jesus, that in the coming ages he might show the immeasurable riches of his grace in the kindness towards us in Christ Jesus. (Eph. 2:4-7)

(F) The sixth idea is to thank God, because He satisfies man with good things as long as he lives. God is a faithful provider for man; He provides man with all good things. However, this divine provision is conditional. Moses said to the people of Israel about the condition of God's care and provision, in these words, which were quoted before:

> And when the LORD your God brings you into the land which he swore to your fathers, to Abraham, to Isaac, and to Jacob, to give you, with great and goodly cities, which you did not build, and houses full of all good things, which you did not fill, and cisterns hewn out, which you did not hew, and vineyards and olive trees, which you did not plant, and when you eat and are full, then take heed lest you forget the LORD, who brought you out of the land of Egypt, out of the house of bondage. You shall fear the LORD your God; you shall serve him, and swear by his name. You shall not go after other gods, of the gods of the peoples who are round about you; for the LORD your God in the midst of you is a jealous God; lest the anger of the LORD your God kindled against you, and destroy you from off the face of the earth. (Deut. 6:10-15)

In these words of Moses, we can see that God provides in abundance to His people when they keep His commandments; but He punishes them for their disobedience.

Joshua, the successor of Moses, conquered the promised land. In his last address to the people of Israel, he reminded them how God kept His promise to them; and exhorted them to serve God faithfully, in these words:

> I gave you a land on which you had not laboured, and cities which you had not built, and you dwell therein; you eat the fruit of vineyard and olive-yards

which you did not plant. Now therefore fear the LORD, and serve him in sincerity and in faithfulness; put away the gods which your fathers served beyond the River, and in Egypt, and serve the LORD. (Jos. 24:13-14)

King David experienced God's constant care and provision for righteous people. He witnessed this fact through these words:

I have been young, and now am old; yet I have not seen the righteous forsaken or his children begging bread. (Ps. 37:25)

Knowing God's faithfulness to His people, Jesus Christ exhorted His followers in these words:

Therefore do not be anxious, saying, 'What shall we eat?' or 'What shall we drink?' or What shall we wear?' For the Gentiles seek all these things; and your heavenly Father knows that you need them all. But seek first his kingdom and his righteousness, and all these things shall be yours as well. (Mt. 6:31-33)

When believers receive all the necessary good things for their life, they should thank God for His constant care and abundant provision.

(G) The seventh idea is a result of the divine providence, which is that man's youth is renewed like eagles. This verse is translated by God's Word Version as follows: "You become young again like an eagle." This translation clarifies the meaning in a better way. In the Bible, an eagle is referred for its strength, in some places (Pr. 30:19; Ezek. 17:3). An extreme length of the eagle's vigorous life was a source of an ancient belief that by an end of certain period, an eagle renews its youth or strength by some unknown means. [5] This belief is mentioned in Ps. 103:5. The intent of the verse is to tell others that God renews strength of the believers, when God forgives all their iniquity, when He heals all their diseases, when He redeems their life from spiritual destruction, when He shows them His steadfast love and mercy, and when He satisfies them with good things throughout their life (Ps. 103:3-5). In other words, God restores physical, mental, and spiritual strength of the believers; God is the source of their life and energy. Because God does these marvellous things for man, man should be thankful to God; and subsequently should praise Him for the benefits, which he has received from God.

Conclusion

As God does all good things to man, man should remember all or at least some benefits and thank God for His steadfast love and mercy. Let his soul be filled with gratitude so that he may praise God, honour Him, and serve Him with sincerity and truth. This is what King David exhorted himself and others to do. We should concur with King David, repeating his words again:

> Bless the LORD, O my soul, and forget not all his benefits, who forgives all your iniquity, who heals all your diseases, who redeems your life from the Pit, who crowns you with steadfast love and mercy, who satisfies you with good as long as you live- so that your youth is renewed like the eagles. (Ps. 103:2-5)

Recommended Hymns from the Methodist Hymnal

12	'Praise my soul, the King of heaven,'
64	'Praise to the Lord, the Almighty,'
233	'Jesus, to Thee we fly,'
726	'Saviour, when in dust to Thee'
851	'All things bright and beautiful,'
920	'Thou to whom the sick and dying'
963	'We plough the fields, and scatter'

Recommended Responsive Readings from the Methodist Hymnal

29 (p. 395),

61 (p. 411)

Recommended Responsive Reading from *A Worship Manual for Scriptural or Methodist Order of Service*

22 (pp. 106-108),

59 (pp. 161-163).

Endnotes

[1] Paul Lee Tan, Encyclopedia of 7700 Illustrations: Sings of the Times, (Rockville, Maryland: Assurance Publishers, Ninth Printing, 1985), # 6593.

[2] *Ibid.,* # 1849.

[3] *Ibid.,* # 1850.

[4] *Ibid.,* # 6580.

[5] Cruden's Complete Concordance to the Old and New Testament by Alexander Cruden, (Ed.) A. D. Adams, C. H. Irwin, S. A. Waters, (Grand Rapids, Michigan: Zondervan Publishing House, Sixteenth Printing, 1976) p. 168.

Chapter 6

Titles of the Sermon

'Liberal Giving Makes Richer,'

'Miser Giving Makes Poorer,'

'Giving as an Index of Prosperity or Poverty'

Scripture

Proverbs 11:17-28

Genesis 14:18-20; 28:22

Leviticus 27:30

Deuteronomy 16:16-17; 26:12-15

I Kings 17:12, 14

Nehemiah 10:18

Malachi 3:7-12

Luke 6:38

I Corinthians 9:6-8

Text: Proverbs 11:24

A Few Versions of the Text, Proverbs 11:24

There is one who scatters, yet increases more; And there is one who withholds more than is right, But it leads to poverty. *The New king James Version*

There is that scattereth, and increases yet more; And there is that withholdeth more than is meet, but it tendeth only to want. *The Wesleyan Bible Commentary*

One man gives freely, yet grows all the richer; another withholds what he should give, and only suffers want. *Revised Standard Version*

One man gives freely, yet gains even more; another withholds unduly, but comes to poverty. *New International Version*

A man may spend freely and yet grow richer; another is sparing beyond measure, yet ends in poverty. *The New English Bible*

It is possible to give away and become richer! It is also possible to hold on too tightly and lose everything. *Then Living Bible Illustrated*

One person spends freely and yet grows richer, while another holds back what he owes and yet grows poorer. *God's Word*

Introduction

Tithing, which means giving to God one tenth of your earning from all sources, is mandatory to all Christian believers, whether they are rich or poor. Tithing is not a matter of ability to afford but is a compliance with God's command to give in accordance with the blessings they received from the LORD God. Giving to God's portion had been a source of blessings to the givers. There are some outstanding persons, who began to tithe when they were poor and because of their giving tithe to God they became rich.

(1) Henry P. Crowell (March 11, 1897- December 10, 1955) had tuberculosis when he was a boy. He could not go to school because of his contagious disease. He went to a church where Rev. Dr. Dwight L. Moody (February 5,1837- December 22,1899), a Methodist preacher, was preaching. He heard God's message through Rev. Moody. Young Crowell prayed saying, "I cannot be a preacher, but I can be a good businessman. God, if you will let me make money, I will use it in your service."

A doctor advised young Crowell to work outdoor. He followed the advice of the doctor; he worked outdoor for seven years and he regained his health.

Crowell brought the little rundown Quaker Mills at Ravana, Ohio. Within ten years, Quaker Oats was a household word to millions. Mr. Crowell was then affectionately called, "The Autocrat of the Breakfast Table."Crowell also opened the huge Perfection Stove.

For forty years Henry P. Crowell faithfully gave 60 to 70% of his income to God's work. We should know that he began to give to God's work his tithe initially and he increased it from 10% to 70%. Crowell has become a rich man by God's blessings upon him. [1]

(2) William Colgate (January 25, 1783-March 25, 1857) left his poor family to earn his living at sixteen. On his way to New York, he met an old canal-boat captain. William told the captain that his father was too poor to keep him and he knew the only trade to make soap and candle. The captain kneeled down and prayed earnestly for the boy and advised him, Someone will soon be the leading soap-maker in New York. It can be you as well as someone else. Be a good man, giving your heart to Christ, pay the Lord all that belongs to Him. Make an honest soap; give a full pound, and I'm certain you 'll be a prosperous and rich man."

William Colgate went to New York in search of a job. He was poor and was feeling lonely. He joined a church. He got a job. When he earned his first dollar, he gave 1/10 to God. He believed that ten cents of every dollar were sacred to the Lord. He faithfully gave 1/10 of every dollar he earned. He had a regular employment. He became a partner of the business of making soap. He later on became the sole owner of the business.

He always remembered the words of the captain. He made an honest soap, gave a full pound. He instructed his bookkeeper to open as account with the Lord of 1/10 of all his income. His business grew rapidly. As he was blessed by the Lord, he increased his giving to the Lord from 1/10 to 2/10, 3/10, 4/10, 5/10 and finally he gave all his income to the Lord's work. He gave millions of dollars to the Lord's work and still remained a rich and prosperous man. [2]

(3) Robert Gilmour LeToureau (November 39,1888- June 1,1969) was a Christian earth-moving machinery manufacturer and a businessman. He pledged to give $ 5,000.00 annually to the Christian and Missionary Alliance Church. During a year of depression, he made $ 35,000.00 profit. But he was puffed up with pride; he withheld his annual payment of $ 5,000.00 to the said church and invested that amount in the business. He anticipated a net profit of $ 100,000.00 in the year. God was not mocked by LeTourneau's withholding his tithe from the storehouse of God. Within a year, his anticipated $ 100,000.00 profit was turned into a $ 100,000.00 loss. He was brought to his knees; he realized that he robbed God of His share. He repented of his deliberate error. He then pledged not only $ 5,000.00 to his church for the year he skipped, but also the same amount for the following year when he was facing a $ 100,000.00 debt and he had no money for payroll. From that point on, LeTourneau's fortune changed. Within four years, he and his wife founded LeTourneau Foundation. The earning of 90% stocks of the Foundation goes to the evangelical Christian work worldwide. The worth of the Foundation was $ 40 million at one time.[3]

Introduction of the Text

These three examples tell us that the persons, who were poor and gave their tithe to the Lord's work became rich. This truth is told to us in the word of God, in the words of the text:

One man gives freely, yet grows all the richer; another withholds what he should give, and only suffers want. (Proverbs 11:24)

This is the text of our meditation now.

The Context of the Text

The text of our meditation is taken from the section which deals with giving away and hoarding basic commodities. When there is a famine in a land, some merchants hoard grain and sell it at a higher price.

When they hide grain from the needy in order to make more and more money or profit, they make making money as their goal. They exploit people and act dishonestly and wickedly. Needy people curse such tradesmen. But the needy bless those who sale grain at a modest price and give grain away in charity. That kind of tradesmen are loved by the people. The liberality of such tradesmen, in the time of crises, makes them good and righteous. Such liberal businessmen proposer. But those tradesmen, who withhold the basic commodities from the people would suffer want. This truth, which is tested and reaffirmed by the people, is stated in the words of the text, as follows:

> One man gives freely, yet grows all the richer; another withholds what he should give, and only suffers want. (Proverbs 11:24)

This is the text within its theological background.

An Analysis of the Text

This text has two ideas. (A) The first idea is about the reason or the key of prosperity, which is "One man gives freely, yet grows all the richer."

(B) The second idea is opposite of the first idea. It is stated as, "another withholds what he should give, and only suffers want."

An Exposition of the Ideas of the Text

As the second idea is contrary to the first idea and it is a negative expression of the first idea, we should meditate on the second idea first

(B) The second idea of the text is opposite of the first idea. It is stated as, "another withholds what he should give, and only suffers want." These words of the text explicitly state two thoughts. (1) The first thought is expressed by the words, "what he should give." It means that a person has a moral responsibility to give to others. (2) The second thought is that the person who fails to give to others only suffers from want.

(1) Let us reflect on the first part of the verse. Everyone is expected to give to others for the welfare or betterment of others. It is a

moral and religious duty to give to others. From a biblical point of view, giving to God's work is a religious obligation, binding all believers. The LORD God spoke to the people of Israel, through Moses:

They shall not appear before the LORD empty-handed; every man shall give as he is able, according to the blessing of the LORD your God which he has given you. (Deut. 16:16-17)

Giving tithes, 1/10 of every thing to God's work was in practice before Moses. Abraham gave his tithe to Melchizedek, the high priest of God (Gen. 14:18-20). Jacob took a vow of giving tithes to God (Gen. 28:22). Following this sacred usage, Moses told the people of Israel: "All the tithe of the land, whether of the seed of the land or of the fruit of the trees, is the LORD's; it is holy to the LORD." (Lev. 27:30) Moses stipulated every third year as the year of tithing. He wrote:

When you have finished paying all the tithes of your produce in the third year, which is the year of tithing, giving it to the Levite, the sojourner, the fatherless, and the widow, that they may eat within your towns and be filled, then you shall say before the LORD your God, 'I have removed the sacred portions out of my house, and moreover I have given it to the Levite, the sojourner, the fatherless, and the widow, according to all thy commandment which thou hast commanded me; I have not transgressed any of thy commandments, neither have I forgotten them... Look down from thy holy habitation, from heaven, and bless the people of Israel and the ground which thou hast given us, as thou didst swear ro our fathers, a land flowing with milk and honey. (Deut. 26:12-15)

We should note that everyone is expected to give tithe to God's work for serving the needs of the unfortunate people such as sojourner, orphans, and widows. The people were asked to give to the Levites who were rendering religious services to them. The Levites were not exempted from tithing. Prophet Nehemiah wrote:

And the priest, the son of Aaron, shall be with the Levites when the Levites receive the tithes; and the Levites shall bring up the tithe of the tithes to the house of our God, to the chambers, the storehouse. (Neh. 10:18)

No minister of a church, however poorly he or she is paid by his or her congregation, is exempted from giving his or her tithes to the Lord God.

(2) Let us now reflect on the second thought which is that the person who fails to give to others only suffers from want. The result of withholding God's portion is to face poverty and scarcity of things. When man withholds God's portion, he breaks the commandment of God; therefore, God does not bless him. When the people of Israel intentionally withheld God's holy portion, God punished them with scarcity, famine, drought, material poverty or want. God spoke to the people of Israel, through prophet Malachi:

> From the days of your father you have turned aside from my statutes and have not kept them. Return to me, and I will return to you, says the LORD of host. But you say, 'How shall we return? Will man rob God?' Yet you are robbing me. But you say, 'How are we robbing thee?' In your tithes and offering. You are cursed with a curse, for you are robbing me, the whole nation of you. (Mal. 3:7-9)

Whenever the people fail to give God's portion, they face God's judgment; they face shortage, want, and poverty, because of the judgment of the LORD God.

(A) Now, we should go on reflecting the first idea of the text. The first idea of the text is about the reason or the key of prosperity, which is "One man gives freely, yet grows all the richer." In other words, a person who gives freely or liberally, or beyond what is expected of him or her, grows richer rather than poor. This idea is a positive expression of giving to God's work. A person who gives more than his or her tithe becomes richer. A liberal giver is blessed by God because God protects his or her crop. This mystery was revealed by God Himself when He spoke through Malachi:

> Bring the full tithes into the storehouse, that there may be food in my house; and thereby put me to the test, says the LORD of hosts; if I will not open the windows of heaven for you and pour down for an overflowing blessing. I will rebuke the devourer for you, so that it will not destroy the fruits of your soil; and your vine in the field shall not fail to bear, says the LORD of host. Then all nations will call you blessed, for you will be a land of delight, says the LORD of host. (Mal. 3:10-12)

These verses explain how liberal givers are made rich and prosperous because God protects their interests and prevents natural calamities causing harm to their produce.

Giving to God's work had been a key of prosperity of man. This point is illustrated by the following event. God asked prophet Elijah to go to Zerapath, when there was drought in Israel. Elijah met a window, gathering sticks. He asked her to bring him water and morsel of bread. The widow replied:

> As the LORD your God lives, I have nothing baked, only a handful of meal in a jar, and a little oil in a cruse; and now, I am gathering a couple of sticks, that I may prepare it for myself and my son, that we may eat it, and die. (I Kg. 17:12)

This was the desperate situation for a family. Prophet Elijah wanted to assure her God's constant care and provision. He said to her:

> Fear not; go and do as you have said; but first make me a little cake of it and bring it to me, and afterward make for yourself and your son. For thus says the LORD the God of Israel, 'the jar of meal shall not be spent, and the cruse of oil shall not fail, until the day that the LORD sends rain upon the earth. (I Kg. 17:14)

The widow did as prophet Elijah asked her to do. She believed in God's promise. Because she obeyed God and gave a portion of her food to God's servant, God blessed her so much as the jar of meal remained filled and the cruse of oil never became empty. This was a miracle. This miracle took place because she gave bread to God's servant first. She did not withhold a portion of God from whatever she had. As she gave the portion to God's servant, she was blessed and she did not face scarcity.

This divine assurance was confirmed by what Jesus Christ said, as follows:

> Give, and it will given you; good measure, pressed down, shaken together, running over, will be put into lap. For the measure you give will the measure you get back. (Lk. 6:38)

In these words, Jesus Christ spoke about the index of giving and receiving. A liberal man gets more liberally in return. The words of an exhortation of St. Paul are very meaningful herein:

> He who sows sparingly will also reap sparingly, and he who sows bountifully will also reap bountifully. Each one must do as he has made up his mind, not reluctantly or under compulsion, for God loves a cheerful giver. And

God is able to provide you with every blessing in abundance, so that you may always have enough of everything and may provide in abundance for every good work. (I Cor. 9:6-8)

Conclusion

The scripture has made very clear to the believers and other people that every person should give to God's work in order to make provisions for sojourners, for orphans, widows, and the servants of the LORD. They have the moral and religious duty to give to God the tithes of everything which they have received from God. They have to give the tithes without compulsion; they should give voluntarily in recognition that God has blessed them. When they give more than their tithes, God blesses them accordingly. He provides them enough of every thing so that they give in abundance for every good work.

Recommended Hymns from the Methodist Hymnal

182   'When I survey the wondrous Cross'

390   'Give me the faith which can remove'

391   'Thy life was given for me,'

394   'Just as I am, Thine own to be,'

399   'What shall I render to my God'

400   'Take my life, and let it be'

573   'O God, what offering shall I give'

Recommended Responsive Reading from the Methodist Hymnal

24 (p. 393)

Recommended Responsive Reading from *A Worship Manual for Scriptural or Methodist Order of Service*

17 (p. 100)

Endnotes

[1] Paul Lee Tan, Encyclopedia of 7700 Illustrations: Signs of the Times, # 1847.

[2] Paul Lee Tan, op. cit., # 1849.

[3] Paul Lee Tan, op. cit., # 1850.

Chapter 7

Titles of the Sermon

'A Prayer of Prophet Habakkuk,'

'Always Thankful to God in Adversities,'

'Unconditional Thanksgiving to the LORD God,'

'Always Rejoicing in the God of Salvation.'

Scripture

Habakkuk 3:1-19

Deuteronomy 11:17

I Kings 4:25

II Kings 18:2-7

Psalms 25:2; 56:3; 20:7-8; 27:3; 46:2

Isaiah 5:19, 12:2;

Haggai 1:6; 2:16

Luke 13:6-9

John 1:48

I Timothy 4:10

I Peter 4:13

Text: Habakkuk 3:17-18

A Few Version of the Text, Habakkuk 3:17-18

Although the fig tree shall not blossom, neither shall fruit be in the vines, the labour of the olive shall fail, and the fields shall yield no meat; the flock shall be cut off from the fold, and there shall be no herd in the stalls: Yet I will rejoice in the LORD, I will joy in the God of my salvation. *King James Version*

Although the fig- tree shall not blossom, neither shall fruit be in the vines, the labor of the olive shall fail, and the fields shall yield no meat, the flock shall be cut off from the fold, and there shall be no herd in the stalls: Yet I will rejoice in Jehovah, I will joy in the God of my salvation. *Explanatory Notes Upon the Old Testament*

Though the fig tree do not blossom, nor fruit be on the vines, the produce of the olive fail and the fields yield no food, the flock be cut off from the fold and there be no herd in the stalls, yet I will rejoice in the LORD, I will joy in the God of my salvation. *Revised Standard Version*

Though the fig tree does not bud and there are no grapes on the vines, though the olive crop fails and the fields produce no food, though there are no sheep in the pen and no cattle herd in the stalls, yet I will rejoice in the LORD. *New International version*

Although the fig-tree does not burgeon, the vines bear no fruit, the olive-crop fails, and the orchards yield no food, the fold is bereft of its flock and there are no cattle in the stalls, yet I will exult in the LORD, rejoice in the God of my deliverance. *The New English Bible*

Even though the fig trees are all destroyed, and there is neither blossom left nor fruit, and though the olive crops all fail, and the fields lie barren; even if the flocks die in the fields and the cattle barns are empty, yet I will rejoice in the Lord; I will be happy in the God of my salvation. *The Living Bible Illustrated*

Even if the fig tree does not bloom and the vines have no grapes, even if the olive tree fails to produce and the fields yield no food, even if the sheep pen is empty and the stalls have no cattle- even then, I will be happy with the LORD, I will truly find joy in the God, who saves me. *God's Word*

Introduction

It is a general trend among the people, including Christians, to thank God whenever they receive blessings from God, in terms of monetary help in financial crises, in terms of recovery from illness, in terms of good news from relatives and friends, in terms of getting new job, in terms of getting promotion, etc. We praise God whenever good things happen to us. We worship God because of His blessings.

Introduction of the Text

The word of God, the Bible, teaches to thank and praise God for His blessings. But it is exceptional to thank and praise God whenever there are calamities in life and scarcities of basic needs. Truly righteous persons thank and praise God in their adversities. For example, prophet Habakkuk prayed to worship and thank God whenever he would face scarcities in his life, when he said:

> **Though the fig tree do not blossom, nor fruit be on the vines, the produce of the olive fail and the fields yield no food, the flock be cut off from the fold and there be no herd in the stalls, yet I will rejoice in the LORD, I will joy in the God of my salvation**. (Habakkuk 3:17-18)

This is the text of our meditation now.

The Context of the Text

Prophet Habakkuk lived and prophesied during the reign of King Manasseh (687-642 B.C.), who reigned forty-five years in Jerusalem. He acted against the will and laws of the LORD God. He rebuilt high places and erected the altars for Baals, and worshiped stars. He burned his sons in sacrifice to these gods and encouraged sorcery. God was angry at King Manasseh because he acted wickedly. He had bad influence on his people; they did worse things than other nations. (II Chr. 33:1-9) The LORD God warned King Manasseh and the people that He would punish them for their wickedness; but they did not pay attention to the warning. Then God sent a commander of the army of the King of Assyria, Esarhaddon (681-669 B.C.) or rather Ashurbanipal (669-626 B.C.) to arrest King Manasseh to carry him to Babylon. While in prison in Babylon, King Manasseh repented of his sins; and God heard his cry and brought him back to Jerusalem. Then King Manasseh realized that the LORD God was true God. Then he carried a reform movement in the kingdom of Judah. He removed idols of other gods and destroyed altars for other gods. He commanded the people to serve the LORD the God of Israel. Nevertheless, the people continued idol worship. (II Chr. 33:14-17)

Prophet Habakkuk saw that the people were not leading just and righteous life. He thought of impending destruction of the kingdom of Judah. He wrote how the LORD God answered to his quarry:

> Write the vision; make it plain upon tablets, so he may run who reads it. For still the vision awaits its time; it hastens to the end-it will not lie. If it seem slow, wait for it; it will surely come, it will not delay. Behold, he whose soul is not upright in him shall fail, but the righteous shall live by his faith. (Hab. 22-4)

Prophet Habakkuk understood God's message that the righteous shall live by his faith whatever might be critical situation. He was convinced of this unshakable faith in the LORD God. With reference to his conviction he wrote the words of our text.

> Though the fig tree do not blossom, nor fruit be on the vines, the produce of the olive fail and the fields yield no food, the flock be cut off from the fold and there be no herd in the stalls, yet I will rejoice in the LORD, I will joy in the God of my salvation. (Habakkuk 3:17-18)

This is the text, within its historical background.

An Analysis of the Text

This text has two main ideas. (A) The first idea is that there would be famine or scarcity of many basic things, such as (1) the fig trees would not blossom, (2) the vines would be without grapes, (3) the olive tree would be without fruit, (4) there would be no crop in the fields, (5) there would be no cattle in the fold, and (6) there would be no herd in the stalls.

(B) The second idea is that despite of these scarcities the man of God would rejoice in the LORD God who would save the godly man.

Exposition of the Ideas of the Text

(A) The first idea is that there would be famine or scarcity of many basic things, such as (1) the fig trees would not blossom, (2) the vines would be without grapes, (3) the olive tree would be without fruit, (4) there would be no crop in the fields, (5) there would be no cattle in the fold, and (6) there would be no herd in the stalls. We shall deal with these details from a biblical point of view.

We should recall that the LORD God brought the people of Israel into a promised land. This good land is described by Moses, who was instrumental to free Hebrews from Egyptian slavery, as follows:

> For the LORD your God is bringing you into a good land, a land of brooks of water, of fountains and springs, flowing forth in valleys and hills, a land of wheat and barley, of vines and fig trees and pomegranates, a land of olive trees and honey, a land in which you will eat bread without scarcity, in which you will lack nothing, a land whose stones are iron, and out of whose hills you can dig copper. And you shall eat and be full, and you shall bless the Lord your God for the good land he has given you. (Deut. 8:7-10)

This promised land, a land of plenty, was given to the people of Israel by the LORD God on a condition that they keep His commandments and statutes. If the people of Israel obey the voice of the LORD God and keep His commandments and statutes, the land would produce plenty of food; and fruit trees would yield plenty. There would be plenty of every needful thing. On the other hand, if the people of Israel disobey the LORD God, the land would cease to produce much; and fruit trees would not yield much. There would be famine and starvation. Not only that, but the people of Israel would be expelled from the promised land; and they would be in exile in the foreign lands and they would perish. (Deut. 8:19-20)

Listen to the words of Moses how the LORD God would bless the people, when they keep His commandments:

> The Lord your God will set you high above all the nations of the earth. And all these blessings shall come upon you and overtake you, if you obey the voice of the LORD your God. Blessed shall you be in the city, and blessed shall you be in the field. Blessed shall be the fruit of your body, and the fruit of your ground, and the fruit of your beasts, the increase of your cattle, and

the young of your flock. Blessed shall be your basket and your kneading-trough. Blessed shall you be when you come in, and blessed shall you be when you go out. (Deut. 28:1-6)

On the other hand, when the people would disobey the LORD God they would be cursed. Moses said to them, as follows:

Cursed shall you be in the city, and cursed shall you be in the field. Cursed shall be your basket and your kneading-trough. Cursed shall be the fruit of your body, and the fruit of your ground, the increase of your cattle, and the young of your flock. Cursed shall you be when you come in, and cursed shall you be when you go out. (Deut. 28:16-19)

Let us go back to the text and examine the scarcities, referred by prophet Habakkuk. The first scarcity is that the fig trees would not blossom. The second scarcity would be that the vines would be without grapes. If there is no blossom, there would be no fruit. This natural principle applies to all fruit bearing trees and plants, for example, tomato, cucumber, mango, apple, orange, grapes, etc.

The Bible speaks of a special significance of fig trees and the vines. They stand for peace and prosperity. About the dominion of King Solomon (962-922 b. C.), a writer of the I Kings wrote as follows:

....he had peace on all sides round about him. And Judah and Israel dwelt in safety, from Dan even to Beer-sheba, every man under his vine and under his fig tree, all the days of Solomon. (I Kg. 14:24-25)

Religious persons used to meditate under the fig tree. Philip brought Nathanael to Jesus Christ. When Nathanael went near Jesus Christ, Jesus Christ complemented him saying, "Behold, an Israelite indeed, in whom is no guile" Nathanael was surprised to hear these words. He asked Jesus Christ, "How do you know me?"Jesus answered him, "Before Philip called you, when you were under the fig tree, I saw you." (Jn 1:47-48)

The third scarcity is that the olive tree would be without fruit. People extract oil from the fruit of olive. This oil is used for cooking. Everybody knows it. Olive oil is an important oil for the Hebrews. The LORD God asked Moses to command the Hebrews to bring pure beaten olive oil for the light that a lamp be set up to burn continually in the tent of meeting and priests were to look after the lamp. This statute was established for all time (Ex.27:20-21). Moreover the olive oil was to be mixed up other spices in order to make a holy anointing oil for anointing the table and utensils, the altars, and priests. It was not to be used for ordinary people. This was the law of the LORD God. (Ex. 30:22-33; 37:29)

The fourth scarcity is that there would be no crop in the fields. Hebrew were planting wheat and barley in the field. These crops were main source of their food. (Deut. 8:8; Ruth 2:2;II Sam.17:28 ;II Chr.2:15;27:5; Job 31:40, etc.)

The fifth and sixth scarcities- (5) there would be no cattle in the fold, and (6) there would be no herd in the stalls. In other words, there would be no domestic animals in the fold and stalls. People get milk products and meat from the domestic animals. These products provide protein to human bodies. Can we imagine breakfast without eggs and milk, and lunch without meat burger, and dinner without roast beef?

(B) The second idea is that despite of these scarcities the man of God would rejoice in the LORD God, who would save the godly man. Let us now summarize the scarcities in order to understand this idea. The scarcities are: 1) the fig trees would not blossom, (2) the vines would be without grapes, (3) the olive tree would be without fruit, (4) there would be no crop in the fields, (5) there would be no cattle in the fold, and (6) there would be no herd in the stalls. In other words, there would be no fruits, no oil, no crop, and no domestic animals. These scarcities occur whenever there is famine and drought. Under this condition, human survival or even existence becomes questionable. A large number of people and animals die of starvation. We have witnessed these horrific scenes in African countries, like Euthopia and Eritrea.

How the godly people should respond when they are faced with famine, drought, scarcities of basic supply for their existence? Should they be sad, despondent, miserable, helpless, and hopeless persons? Or should they be content, happy, and hopeful? What the word of God, the Bible has to say?

When Hebrews were passing through the wilderness, the LORD God made them hungry; and they asked for bread to Moses. God fed them with manna, a food from the sky, for those forty years. The purpose of this divine provision was that man should know that he does not live by bread alone, but he lives by everything that proceeds out of the mouth of the LORD. (Deut. 8:3)

Jesus Christ was taken in the wilderness to be tempted by the devil. Jesus Christ did not eat food for forty days and forty nights. He was feeling hungry. At that moment, the tempter said to Jesus Christ to command the stones to become loaves of bread. In reply, Jesus Christ quoted the above mentioned verse, "Man shall not live by bread alone, but by every word that proceeds from the mouth of God." (Mt. 4:4)

The LORD God asked prophet Elijah to see King Ahab (869-850 B. C.), the king of Israel, and to declare that there would be no rain for some years, except by the word of the LORD. Then the LORD God asked Elijah to hide himself by the brook Cherith, which was east of Jordan. As there was famine in Israel, there was a scarcity of food. God commanded ravens to take bread and meat in the morning and in the evening to Elijah. Elijah used to drink water from the brook; and ravens were supplying him bread and meat every day. (I Kg. 17:1-6) Afterwards, God commanded a widow from Zarephath to feed Elijah; the jar of her meal and cruse of oil remained filled all the days, because God wanted to provide food to His servant, Elijah. (I Kg. 17:8-16)

Godly person must have trust in the LORD God that He would provide for his survival, therefore he or she should not be anxious over his or her basic needs. Jesus Christ taught the people not be anxious about food, drink, and clothes; they should have faith in God. He said to them:

> Therefore do not be anxious, saying, 'What shall we eat?' Or 'What shall we drink?' Or 'What shall we wear?' For the Gentiles seek these things; and your heavenly Father knows that you need them all. But seek first his kingdom and his righteousness, and all these things shall be yours as well. (Mt. 6:31-33)

The Book of Job narrated us that Job was blameless and upright; he feared God and turned away from evil. He had seven sons and three daughters. He had 7,000 sheep, 3,000 camels, 1,000 oxen, 500 she-asses. He had many servants. He was the greatest of the people of the east. (Jo 1:1-3)

Satan argued with God saying that God protected Job and caused him to prosper. If God would remove all his possessions, Job would curse God. God allowed Satan to take away the possessions of Job. A servant of Job reported that his oxen and asses were taken by Sabeans; and his servants were killed by their swords. Another servant told Job that his sheep and servants were destroyed by fire from heaven. Another servant reported that his camels were taken away by Chaldeans; and his servants were killed by swords. Another servants reported that his sons and daughters were killed when the house was destroyed by tornado. (Job 1:13-19)

When Job heard these losses and calamities, he fell upon the ground and worshiped God. In that hour, he said very memorable words, as follow:

> Naked I came from my mother's womb, and naked shall I return; the LORD gave, and the LORD has taken away; blessed be the name of the LORD. (Job 1:21)

Job did not blame God for his losses; but he worshiped God. He knew that all are perishable. He did not lose his trust in God.

Some psalm writers expressed their confidence in the LORD God, saying:

> Though a host encamp against me, my heart shall not fear; though war arise against me, yet I will be confident. (Ps. 27:3)

> God is our refuse and strength, a very pleasant help in trouble. Therefore we will not fear though the earth should change, though the mountains shake in the heart of the sea; though its waters roar and foam, the mountains tremble with its tumult. (Ps. 46:1-3)

Like Job, prophet Isaiah said:

> Behold, God is my salvation; I will trust, I will not be afraid; for the LORD is my strength and my song, and he has become my salvation. (Is. 12:2)

The same confidence in God was expressed by the apostles of Jesus Christ. St Paul wrote to Timothy, saying:

> Having nothing to do with godless and silly myths, train yourself in godliness; for while bodily training is of some value, godliness is of value in every way, as it holds promise for the present life and also for the life to come. This saying is sure and worthy of full acceptance. For to this end we toil and strive, because we have our hope set on the living God, who is the Saviour of all men, especially for those who believe. (I Tim. 4:7-10)

Conclusion

Prophet Habakkuk, Job, psalm writers, and apostle Paul had trust or confidence in God when they confronted calamities and scarcities of life. They worshiped God and praised Him. Worshiping and praising the LORD God should be unconditional. The entire Bible teaches the believers that they should not lose heart; but have trust in God because He protects and provides to those who firmly believe in Him. If they have such a firm faith and conviction in God's providence, they should worship and praise God in all conditions.

Recommended Hymns from the Methodist Hymnal

10   'Now thank we all our God,'

634   'Will your anchor hold in the'

962   'Come, ye thankful people, come,'

963   'We plough the fields, and scatter'

Recommended Responsive Reading from A Worship Manual for a Scriptural or Methodist Order of Service

\# 17 (p. 100),

\# 26 (pp. 112-113),

\# 106 (pp.246-248).

Chapter 8

Titles of the Sermon

'Greater Splendour of God's Temple,'

'Second Temple of God and His Two Promises,'

'Two Promises of God, Accompanied with Building the Second Temple for God,'

'Prosperity Because of Priority to God's Work.'

Scripture

Haggai 2:1-9

I Kings 6:1-38; 7:13-51; 8:35-36

II Kings 24:12

II Chronicles 36:10

Ezra 1:1; 2:1, 5, 64; 4:24; 6;3-5, 8, 15

Nehemiah 2:1

Isaiah 45:3

Jeremiah 52:28-29

Haggai 1:1, 15; 2:10, 20

Malachi 3:8-11

Matthew 6:32-33

Text: Haggai 2:9

A Few Versions of the Text, Haggai 2:9

The glory of this latter temple shall be greater than the former,' says the LORD of hosts. 'And in this place I will give peace,' says the LORD of hosts. *The New King James Version*

The latter glory of this house shall be greater than the former,' saith Jehovah of hosts; and in this place will I give peace,' saith Jehovah of hosts. *The Wesleyan Bible Commentary*

The latter splendour of this house shall be greater than the former, says the LORD of hosts; and in this place I will give prosperity, says the LORD of hosts. *Revised Standard Version*

The glory of this present house will be greater than the glory of former house,' says the LORD Almighty. 'And in this place I will grant peace,' declarers the LORD Almighty. *New International Version*

And the glory of this latter house shall surpass the glory of the former,' says the LORD of Hosts. In this place will I grant prosperity and peace. This is the very word of the LORD of Hosts. *The New English Bible*

The future splendour of this Temple will be greater than the splendour of the first one! For I have plenty of silver and gold to do it! And here I will give peace,' says the LORD. *The Living Bible Illustrated*

This new house will be more glorious than the former, declares the LORD of Armies. And in this place I will give [them] peace,' declares the LORD of Armies. *God's Word*

Introduction

Most of the Christian denominations have been facing financial and managerial crises, because Christians do not go to churches regularly. They have stopped supporting the churches financially and rendering voluntary services. Many church buildings are abandoned, neglected, and sold to other religious groups; and some church buildings are demolished because Christians lost interest in public worship and in their commitment to support God's work.

Many Christians are showing apathy toward church buildings because their lifestyle is changed. Many of them work on Saturdays and on Sundays for livelihood. When they work hard on weekend, they choose Sunday a day to relax and to entertain. Some choose to work on the weekend because they get more wages than wages for regular days. It is a part of their greed. Christians do not give priority to worship God on Sunday and to support their churches financially.

Many Christians are poor; and some are living on social welfare. They live in developed and affluent countries, like U. S. A. and Canada. Yet these affluent countries have many people, living below poverty line. Children born of poor parents have to live in poverty. They do not get enough food to eat; they starve sometimes. Some schools provide breakfast to children. They do not have enough clothing. Some children live on the streets, because their parents had abandoned them.

Poverty in affluent countries is a puzzle for many thinking persons. Providing things in plenty to the poor would not solve the problem. The solution lies in teaching Christian values to the people that they turn to God in Jesus Christ; and attend public serves on Sundays and give in charity. Then the LORD God would bless them abundantly; God would make them prosperous and content. This is a spiritual solution to the problem of poverty in the affluent lands.

Introduction of the Text

The word of God addressed the problem of poverty and scarcity, when the LORD God inspired prophet Haggai, to exhort the Jews, upon their return from the exile:

Consider how you have fared. You have sown much, and harvested little. You eat, but you never have enough; you drink, but you never have your fill; you clothe yourselves, but no one is warm; and he who earns wages earns wages to put them into a bag with holes... You have looked for much, and lo, it came to little; and when you brought it home, I blew it away. Why? says the LORD of hosts. Because of my house that lies in ruins, while you busy yourselves each with his own house. Therefore the heavens above you have withheld the dew, and the earth has withheld its produce. And I have called you for a drought upon the land and the hills, upon the grain, and the new wine, the oil, upon what the ground bring forth, upon men and cattle, and upon all their labors. (Hag. 1:5-11)

As the Jews, who returned from Babylon to Jerusalem and Judah, and who were busy with building houses for themselves, neglected the work of building the second temple for the LORD God, God withheld His blessing from them; therefore, they had want of every thing. It was the LORD God who inspired the Persian rulers to issue decrees, allowing the Jews to return to Jerusalem and Judah to build the temple for the LORD God. Upon their arrival, they forgot God's work and gave priority to their personal well-being. Therefore, God sent prophet Haggai, with the message that they should give priority to God's work; and God promised them two things if they would build the second temple. Haggai gave God's message to the Jews, as follows:

The latter splendour of this house shall be greater than the former, says the LORD of hosts; and in this place I will give prosperity, says the LORD of hosts. (Haggai 2:9)

This is the text of our meditation now.

The Context of the Text

The LORD God spoke these words of the text to the people of Judah, through prophet Haggai. Let us know the historical background of the text. Cyrus (539-530 B. C.) a Persian king, issued an edict for the return of the Jews in ca. 538 B. C. (Ezra 1:1) Accordingly a few leaders of the Jews returned to Jerusalem. (1) Zerubbabel, the governor of Judah (538-445 B.C.), undertook to restore the temple in ca. 537 B. C. (Ezra (3:8), on the second year after his return. The work was interrupted (Ezra 4:5, 24). (2) Joshua came with Zerubbabel. (Ezra 2:2) He became the high priest in Jerusalem. (3) Nehemiah came with Zerubbable (Ezra 2:2). He was the cupbearer of the Persian King Artaxerxes I (465-424 B. C.) (Ezra 2:1; Hag. 1:1; Neh. 2:1). After Zeruabbable, Nehemiah became governor of Judah (445-433 B.C.) (Neh. 2:1; 5:14) (4) Ezra, who was a priest and a scribe (Neh. 8:9), returned to Jerusalem in ca. 458 B. C. (Ezra 7:7) These leaders were the contemporaries of prophet Haggai. (Ezra 5:1-2) These four leaders were involved in rebuilding the temple of God at Jerusalem and in repairing the walls of Jerusalem.

We should know a brief history of the event of Babylonian captivity. Nebuchadnezzar (605-562 B. C.) defeated the kingdoms of Israel and Judah and took 3, 023 Jews o Babylon (Jer. 52:28) in captivity in ca. 599 B. C. During the reign of Jehoiakim (609-598 B. C.), he took some more Jews in captivity in ca. 598 B. C. (II Kg. 24:12; II Chr. 36:10). During the reign of King Jehoichin (598 B. C.), he deported 832 persons from Jerusalem in ca. 588 B. C. (Jer. 52:29). He again deported 745 Jews in ca. 583 B. C. (Jer. 52:20). The Jews were in exile from 587 to 539 B. C., for forty-eight years. The Babylonian empire was overthrown by King Cyrus (559-530 B. C) of Persia in 539 B. C. Prophet Isaiah spoke of King Cyrus as God's anointed to accomplish God's plan (Is. 45:3). King Cyrus issued an edict for the return of the Jews in ca. 538 B. C. (Ezra 1:1) After King Cyrus, Darius the Great (522-486 B. C.) came in power. King Darius was well disposed toward the Jews. He decreed the Jews to return to their motherland in 536 B. C. According to the record of Ezra, 42, 360 Jews returned to Jerusalem and Judah (Ezra 2:64). They started to build the second temple of the LORD God in 534 B.C., two years after they settled in the land. The work of building the second temple was going on very slowly because the Jews gave priority to build houses for themselves first; and they were saying among themselves that the time had not yet come to rebuild the house of the LORD God. They were busy with building goodly houses for themselves; and they had no time to rebuild the temple. Jews lost zeal for God's work because of their materialistic thinking. The work on rebuilding the temple consequently stopped for about fourteen years.

After those fourteen years' neglect, God spoke to the leaders of Judah through prophet Haggai. Haggai spoke to Zerubbabel, the governor of Judah, Joshua, the high priest, and the people of Jerusalem. He spoke to them while they were observing the Feast of Tabernacle (Lev. 23:33-43). He prophesied between September and December of 520 B. C. (Hag. 1:1; 2:1, 10, 20)[1]

Prophet Haggai challenged the Jews to be strong or firm, because the Spirit of the LORD God abided in them (Hag. 2:5). He told them that a man of average ability, who is fully dedicated to God, can accomplish much under the anointing of the Spirit of God. He spoke to them two promises of God, if they would rebuild the house of God, saying:

> The latter splendour of this house shall be greater than the former, says the LORD of hosts; and in this place I will give prosperity, says the LORD of hosts. (Haggai 2:9)

This is the text, within its historical setting.

Because of the preaching of prophet Haggai, the work on rebuilding the house of the LORD God was resumed in 520 B. C. (Ezra 4:24; Hag. 1:15) The work was completed in ca. 516 B. C. (Ezra 6:15), in the sixth year of King Darius I (522-486 B. C.). It took more than thirty years to complete the work on the second temple. This second temple was completed and dedicated while King Darius the Great was ruling. This second temple was called Zerubbabel's temple, because Zerubbabel, the governor of Judah, undertook to restore the temple in ca. 537 B..C., two years after his return.

An Analysis of the Text

This text has two ideas. (A) The first idea is the first promise of the LORD God about the temple that the splendour of the second temple would be greater than the former temple.

(B) The second idea is the second promise of the LORD God that He would give the Jews prosperity in the place or in the temple.

An Exposition of the Ideas of the Text

(A) The first idea of the text is the first promise of the LORD God about the temple that the splendour of the second temple would be greater than the former temple.

We should recall that the first temple of the LORD God was built by King Solomon (962-922 B. C.). He began to build the first temple in 957 B. C. The work was completed after seven years (I Kg. 6:38). The temple was very large and beautiful. The dimensions of the temple are given in I Kg. 6:1-38; 7:13-51. It was sixty cubits long (90'), twenty cubits wide (30'), and thirty cubits high (45'). (I Kg. 6:2) One cubit is 1'.6". The second temple was built by governor Zerubbabel and the Jews who returned from the exile. They spent thirty years on building the second temple. The dimensions of the temple are given in Ezra 6:4. Its height was 60 cubits (90'); its width was 60 cubits (90'). Its length is not mentioned by Ezra. The second temple was 60' wider and 45' higher than the first temple.

The second temple was built according to the decree of King Cyrus of Persia (539-530 B. C.) It was built with all golden and silver things of the first temple, which Nebuchadnezzar (605-562 B. C.) took out of the temple. King Cyrus returned those things to Jerusalem (Ezra 6:3-5). All expenses of building the temple were paid through the royal treasure (Ezra 6:8). Therefore, the splendour of the second temple was greater than the former temple, built by King Solomon (962-922 B. C.) When the Jews completed the second temple of the LORD God, its glory was greater than the first temple. The promise of the LORD God was fulfilled when the second temple was built.

(B) The second idea of the text is the second promise of the LORD God that He would give the Jews prosperity in the place or in the temple. It means that if Jews would build the temple for the LORD God, He would make them prosperous. God promised them prosperity on a condition. They would have enough food to eat, enough water to drink, enough clothes to keep them warm. They would not have wants of shortages of their basic supply.

Prosperity, peace, and happiness depend on the grace of God. These blessings are conditional. Let us see how those blessings were conditional since King Solomon (962-922 B. C.) built the first temple.

King Solomon dedicated the temple to the LORD God; and he prayed to God for various conditional blessings. With reference to rain and prosperity, he prayed:

> When heaven is shut up and there is no rain because they sinned against thee, if they pray toward this place, and acknowledge thy name, and turn from their sin, when thou dost afflict them, then hear thou in heaven, and forgive the sin of the servants, thy people Israel, when thou dost teach them the good way in which they should walk; and grant rain upon the land, which thou hast given to thy people as an inheritance. (I Kg. 8:35-36)

This portion of King Solomon's prayer tells us again that God controls rain; and He grants prosperity to the repentant people again.

Material prosperity is dependent on the condition, when the people give to God's work generously and when they give tithes to God's work as the minimum thanksgiving to God. The LORD God made this idea very clear to the people of Israel, through prophet Malachi, in the following words:

> Will man rob God? Yet you are robbing me. But you say, 'How are we robbing thee?' In your tithes and offerings. You are cursed with a curse, for you are robbing me; the whole nation of you. Bring the full tithes into the storehouse, that there may be food in my house; and thereby put me to the test, says the LORD of hosts, if I will not open the windows of heaven for you and pour down for you an overflowing blessing. I will rebuke the devourer for you, so that it will not destroy the fruits of your soil; and your vine in the field shall not fail to bear, says the LORD of hosts. (Mal. 3:8-11)

When the Jews returned from Babylon to Jerusalem, they neglected building the temple for the LORD God; and they were facing wants. In the context of the scarcity of the needful things, God said to the Jews, through Haggai:

> Because of my house lies in ruins, while you busy yourselves each with his own house. Therefore the heavens above withheld the dew, and the earth has withheld its produce. (Hag. 1:9-10)

These verses mean that God controls rain and produce of the earth. He would cause to rain fall and the earth to yield produce, if the people give the tithes to the LORD God.

People have to give priority to God's work and His concerns over their concerns. When they would do thus, God would make them prosperous. With reference to this, Jesus Christ taught His disciples, saying:

> But seek first his kingdom and his righteousness, and these things shall be yours as well. (Mt. 6:33)

God would give other things to the believers because He knows that His children need those things (Mt. 6:32). Believers should not seek the worldly things first; but they should seek God's kingdom and His righteousness first.

Conclusion

The text of our meditation today reveals to us the secret of prosperity and peace and contentment. When we give priority to God's work in our life, God blesses our resources of a livelihood. He grants us prosperity and peace from His temple. The believers should know this key of peace and prosperity; therefore, they should give priority to seeking God's kingdom and His righteousness; and then all other things would be added to them.

Recommended Hymns from the Methodist Hymnal

7   'Heavenly King, look down from above;'

669   'Dear Lord and Father of mankind,'

677   'We love the place, O God,'

692   'O Saviour, bless us ere we go;'

Recommended Responsive Reading from the Methodist Hymnal

43 (p. 402) or

58 (p. 409)

Recommended Responsive Reading from *A Worship Manual for Scriptural or Methodist Order of Service*

37 (pp.129-130) or

56 (pp. 157-158).

Endnotes

[1] The Wesleyan Bible Commentary, Vol. III, p. 741.

Chapter 9

Titles of the Sermon
'Returning to Thank God in Jesus Christ,'
'Returning to Praise God,'
'A Sense of Gratitude in a Foreigner,'
'Forgetting to Praise God.'

Scripture
Luke 17:11-19
Leviticus 13:43-46; 14:2-32
Numbers 5:2-4
Deuteronomy 6:10-12; 8:11-18
II Kings 5:15-19
Psalms 103:1-5
Matthew 8:4
Mark 1:44
Luke 5:14
I Thessalonians 5:18

Text: Luke 17:18

A Few Versions of the Text, Luke 17:18
Were there not any found who returned to give glory to God except this foreigner? *The New King James Version*

There are not found returning to give glory to God, save this stranger.
Explanatory Notes Upon the New Testament

Was no one found to return and give praise to God except this foreigner?
Revised Standard Version

Was no one found who to return to give praise to God except this
foreigner? *New International Version*

Could none be found to come back and give praise to God except this
foreigner? *The New English Bible*

Does only this foreigner return to give glory to God? *The Living Bible
Illustrated*

Only this foreigner came back to praise God. *God's Word*

Introduction

(1) It is very appropriate to begin a Thanksgiving Day service with the
following hymn:

Now thank we all our God
With hearts, and hands, and voices;
Who wondrous things hath done,
In whom His world rejoices;
Who, from our mothers' arms,
Hath blessed us on our way
with countless gifts of love,
And still is ours to day.   1
O may this bounteous God
Through all our life be near us,
With ever-joyful hearts
And blessed peace to cheer us,
And keep us in His grace,
And guide us when perplexed,
And free us from all ills
In this world and the next.   2
All praise and thanks to God
The Father now be given,

The Son and Him who reigns

With them in highest heaven;

The one, eternal God,

Whom earth and heaven adore;

For thus it was, in now,

And shall be evermore.   3[1]

This popular hymn was written by Rev. Martin Rinkart (April 23, 1586-December 8, 1649). He was born on April 23, 1586 in Eilenberg, Saxony, Germany. He was an ordained minister of the Luthern Church. He was called to be the pastor in his native town of Eilenberg. He arrived there just when the dreadful bloodshed was starting. Eilenberg was a walled city; therefore, many political and military fugitives took refuge in the city. The city witnessed the Thirty Years' War (1618-1648). Throughout these war years there were several deadly pestilence and famines. Rev. Martin Rinkart's home served as a refuge for the afflicted victims. The plague of 1637 was very severe. Rev. Martin Rinkart was the only remaining minister in the city, daily conducting as many as fifty funeral services.

During the closing years of war, Eilenberg was overrun by invading armies on three different occasions- once by the Austrian army and twice by the Swedish army. During one of the occupations by the Swedish army, there came the demand to pay a large tribute by those impoverished people. Rev. Rinkart interceded with the leaders of the army to reduce the tribute. But the Swedish commander would not at first consider Rev. Rinkart's request. Then Rev. Rinkart said to his parishioners, "Come, my children, we can find no mercy with man; let us take refuge with God." He led the people in prayer and in signing. The spiritual fervency moved the Swedish commander to lower the demands of the tribute payment. [2]

This hymn tells us how Rev. Rinkart thanked God for His continued care in crises.

(2) Rev. John Wesley (June 17, 1703- March 2, 1791) met a porter of his college at Oxford in 1725. He said to the porter: "You thank God when you have nothing to wear, nothing to eat, and no bed

to lie upon; what else do you thank Him for?" The porter replied: "I thank Him that he has given me my life and being, a heart to love Him, and a desire to serve Him." These words of sincere gratitude to God made Rev. John Wesley to feel that there was something in religion, which he had not as yet found. He began to search for a religious conviction.[3] The grateful attitude of the poor porter motivated Rev. John Wesley to find in Christianity why some Christians have religious conviction.

Introduction of the Text

These aforesaid examples teach the believers to thank God and praise Him in all circumstances as St. Paul exhorted Christians at Thessalonia (I Thes. 5:18). It is a virtue to thank God for His favours and to glorify Him for His blessings. But there are many people, who take blessings for granted, and they subsequently fail to thank God and praise Him. This fact of our life is told to us in a form of the question, which Jesus Christ asked the crowd, in these words:

> **Was no one found to return and give praise to God except this foreigner? (Lk. 17:18)**

This is the text of our meditation now.

The Context of the Text

Jesus Christ and His disciples had to pass through a village, which was situated between Samaria and Galilee. As they reached the border of the village, ten lepers came to meet Jesus Christ. Nine of them were Jews; and one was a Samaritan, a foreigner. These lepers were staying together in a colony, outside the village. The Jews had no dealings with Samaritans, who were outcast people. But the common misery of leprosy made them forget their differences; therefore, they were staying together in the colony of lepers. An existence of a similar colony is mentioned in II Kings 7:3.

According to the Jewish law, leprosy makes persons unclean. This was the law for lepers, as follows:

> The leper who has the disease shall wear torn clothes and let the hair of his head hang loose, he shall cover his upper lip and cry, ' unclean, unclean.' He

shall remain unclean as long as he has the disease; he is unclean; he shall dwell alone in a habitation outside the camp. (Lev. 13:45-46 cf. Num. 5:2-4)

When those lepers somehow came to know that Jesus Christ was going to pass through the village, they came out of their colony. They stood at a distance, about fifty yards away. They lifted up their voices and cried aloud: "Jesus, Master, have mercy on us." (Lk. 17:13) They must have kept shouting until Jesus paid attention to them. When Jesus Christ saw them, He had compassion on them (Mk. 1:41). He said to them, "Go and show yourselves to the priests." (Lk. 17:14) Jesus Christ said to them to do so, in accordance with the Jewish law. According to the Jewish law, when a person is cured of leprosy, he had to go to a priest for examination that he was truly clean. Then he had to offer a sacrifice to God and do other ceremonial things (Lev. 14:2-32). On other occasions, when Jesus Christ healed lepers He asked them to do the needful as prescribed by Moses (Lk. 5:14; Mt. 8:4; Mk 1:44).

Those ten lepers believed in Jesus Christ and obeyed His command. As they were on their way to show themselves to priests, one of them realized that he was healed of leprosy. He was a Samaritan, a foreigner. He turned back to Jesus Christ, praising God with a loud voice. But other nine lepers, who were Jews, continued their journey to show themselves to priests that they were cured of leprosy. Having shown themselves to priests, they did not turn back to see Jesus Christ; and thank Him and to praise God for the miraculous healing. When the Samaritan returned to Jesus Christ, he fell on his face at Jesus' feet and gave Jesus Christ thanks repeatedly. Then Jesus Christ asked questions to those who were around him: "Were not ten cleansed? Where are the nine? Was no one found to return and give praise to God except this foreigner? "(Lk. 17:17-18) These questions imply that all ten lepers were healed on their way to priests. But all of them did not return to give praise to God, except the Samaritan, a foreigner. "Was no one found to return and give praise to God except this foreigner? " (Lk. 17:18) is one of those questions. This is the text of our mediation, within its context.

An Analysis of the Text

The text, "Was no one found to return and give praise to God except this foreigner? " (Lk. 17:18) points out two different ways, the people respond to God's blessings.

(A) The first way of responding to God's blessing is not to return to Jesus Christ and praise God in the presence of others. The nine Jews, after the miraculous recovery, did not find time to return to Jesus Christ, at whose command they were healed. In other words, we have to reflect on the question, "Why did the Jews fail to thank Jesus Christ and to praise God?"

(B) The second way of responding to God's blessing is to return to Jesus Christ and to thank God and to praise Him in the presence of others. The Samaritan, a foreigner, followed the right way. In other words, we have to reflect on the question, "Why did the Samaritan act rightly and exceptionally?"

Exposition of the Ideas of the Text

(A) The first idea of the text is the first way of responding to God's blessing in terms of not returning to Jesus Christ and praising God in the presence of others. The first derived question would be "Why did the Jews fail to thank Jesus Christ and to praise God?"

The Samaritan leper, when he saw at himself and others, while on their way to show them to priests, that they were cured of leprosy, he must have told his fellows that he was going back to Jesus Christ to thank Him and to praise God. The Jews, who were healed of leprosy, saw him returning to Jesus Christ; but they had no desire and intention to return to Jesus Christ. They avoided seeing Jesus Christ after their being united with their relatives and friends. They might have told their close friends how they were healed; but they have no courage to tell others publicly that they were healed at the command of Jesus Christ. If they had done so, the gospel writers would have recorded their witness. They failed to bear witnesses individually and collectively that Jesus Christ cured them of leprosy. They knew that they would have been considered as followers of Jesus Christ and they could have been expelled by the Jewish authority. They were not ready to pay such dearly social cost.

We should remind ourselves of how they asked Jesus to be merciful to them. As they were isolated from their families and friends because of their leprosy, they knew the pain of being outcast and of physical sickness. They had a strong desire to be united with their society; they were ready to do at any cost. They humbled themselves and cried for the mercy of Jesus Christ. Jesus Christ showed compassion to them. He healed them instantly and asked them to show themselves to the priests. But they did not realize that they were healed instantly. They must have realized that all of them were healed when the Samaritan told them that he was going back to Jesus to thank Him. The nine Jews went ahead to show themselves to the priests and do required rituals before they were allowed to be reunited with the society. In their joy of their social unification, they forgot to give thanks to Jesus Christ and praise God in the presence of others. They showed ingratitude to Jesus Christ by not returning to him.

It is a human tendency to forget benefactors and to credit oneself of achievements. It is likely that they must have taken a credit to themselves that they shouted so loudly and made Jesus to pay attention to them or that they were very tactful to force Jesus to be compassionate to them. Moses warned against this human tendency when he said to the people of Israel:

> Take heed lest you forget the LORD your God, by not keeping his commandments and his ordinances and his statutes, which I command you this day: Lest, when you have eaten and are full, and have built goodly houses and live in them, and when your herds and flock multiply, and your silver and gold is multiplied, and all that you have is multiplied, then your heart be lifted up, and you forget the LORD your God, who brought you out of the land of Egypt, out of the house of bondage, who led you through the great and terrible wilderness, with its fiery serpents and scorpions and thirsty ground where there was no water, who brought you water out of the flinty rock, who fed you in the wilderness with manna which your fathers did not know, that he might humble you and test you, to do you good in the end. Beware lest you say in your heart, 'My power and the might of my hand have gotten me this wealth. You shall remember the LORD your God, for it is

he who gives you power to get wealth; that he may confirm his covenant which he swore to your fathers, as at this day.' (Deut. 8:11-18 cf. Deut. 6:10-12)

The history of the Jews, which is recorded in the Bible, teaches us that the Jews forgot God many times; and they worshipped other gods. They often forgot how God redeemed them from various crises. God punished them for their sins against Him; however, they did not remember the benefits they received at His hand.

(B) The second idea of the text is the second way of responding to God's blessing in terms of returning to Jesus Christ and thanking God and praising Him in the presence of others. The Samaritan, a foreigner, followed the right way. In other words, we have to reflect on the question, "Why did the Samaritan act rightly and exceptionally?"

When the Samaritan saw himself and others that they all were cured of leprosy on their way to show themselves to priests, he returned to Jesus, praising God with a loud voice. When he met Jesus Christ, he humbled himself before Him in the presence of a crowd; he fell on his face at Jesus' feet and gave Him thanks. He continued to praise God with loud voice, in the presence of others. As he shouted for mercy and compassion of Jesus while he was a leper, he shouted to praise God when he was cured of leprosy. He did not imitate the other nine Jews who went to the priests and to be reunited with their society; he did not follow the crowd but he took an exceptional and right way. After being healed, he did not go to his families and friends first; but he went back to Jesus Christ, by whose word he was made whole. He did not forget his benefactor; he went back to Jesus Christ to thank Him personally and to praise God for the gift of healing. He appreciated goodness of God in Jesus Christ. Even though he was a foreigner, a Samaritan, he knew how to remember his benefactor and how to express his gratitude in humility. He had a right spirit and a right attitude toward God. King David spoke of this spirit in a psalm, as follows:

Bless the LORD, O my soul; and all that is within me, bless his holy name!
Bless the LORD, O my soul, and forget not all his benefits, who forgives

all your iniquity, who heals all your diseases, who redeems your life from the
Pit, who crowns you with steadfast love and mercy, who satisfies you with
good as long as you live so that your youth is renewed like the eagle's.
(Ps. 103:1-5)

The Samaritan, who went back to Jesus Christ to thank Him and to
praise God, should remind us of another foreigner, a Syrian called
Naaman, who was healed from leprosy by prophet Elisha. When
Naaman was cured of leprosy, he and his company returned to prophet
Elisha to thank Elisha and to praise God. He stood before Elisha and
said: "Behold, I know that there is no God in all the earth but in Israel;
so accept now a present from your servant." (II Kg. 5:15) Prophet
Elisha said, "As the LORD lives, whom I serve, I will receive none."
(II Kg.5:16) Naaman urged him to take the gift; but Elisha refused to
take anything from him. Then Naaman humbled himself and requested
another favour of the prophet, saying:

> If not, I pray to you, let there be given your servant two mule's burden of
> earth; for henceforth your servant will not offer burnt offering or sacrifice to
> any god but the LORD. In this matter may the LORD pardon your servant:
> When my master goes into the house of Rimmon to worship there, leaning
> on my arm, and I bow myself in the house of Rimmon, when I bow myself
> in the house of Rimmon, the LORD pardon your servant in this matter.
> (II Kg. 5:17-18)

Then Eisha said to Naaman, 'Go in peace.' Naaman must have praised
God for the cure; and he promised to be faithful to the LORD God.

Conclusion
In the event of healing the ten lepers, there are two ways of responding
to God's blessings. Majority of the people forget to give thanks to
God and to praise Him, when He heals them from sickness or rescues
them from crises. They take God's blessing for granted. When they are
saved from desperation and difficulties, they may not thank God
individually; and they do not praise God for His blessings in the
presence of other believers and nonbeliever. It is wrong attitude to
forget God and the benefactors. Jesus Christ did not approve this
attitude. The Samaritan, a foreigner, who was healed by Jesus Christ,

went back to Jesus Christ to thank Him and to praise God in the presence of others. He showed the right attitude and the right way how to appreciate God's grace and His kind works.

The Samaritan is a special example to many Canadians, who immigrated to Canada and who are blessed by God in various ways. They should recall the adverse conditions -political, social, and economical, which were obstacles in the way of their material, social, religious, and political progress and prosperity. When they settled in Canada and God opened a better way of life, they should thank God and praise Him.

May God grant this understanding to all Christians when they celebrate this Thanksgiving Day. God in Jesus Christ will be pleased with His people, when they show the right attitude toward Him.

Recommended Hymns from the Methodist Hymnal

10   'Now thank we all our God,'

12   'Praise, my soul, the King of heaven,'

64   'Praise to the Lord, the Almighty,'

524   'My God, I thank Thee, who hast made'

550   'O For a heart to praise my God,'

851   'All things bright and beautiful,'

963   'We plough the fields, and scatter'

968   'Yes, God is good- in earth and sky,'

969   'O Lord of heaven and earth and sea,'

Recommended Responsive Readings from the Methodist Hymnal

29 (p. 395),

51 (p. 406),

61 (p. 411).

Recommended Responsive Readings from *A Worship Manual for Scriptural or Methodist Order of Service*

22 (pp.106-108),

48 (pp.145-147),

59 (pp.161-163).

Endnotes

[1] The Methodist Hymn-Book, (London: the Methodist Publishing House, Revised 1954) # 10.

[2] Kenneth W. Osbeck, 101 Hymns Stories, (Grand Rapids, Michigan: Kergel Publications, 1982), pp. 173-174.

[3] Methodist Preacher, John Wesley the Methodist: A Plain Account of His Life and Work, (New York: Eaton & Mains, 1903), p. 55.

Chapter 10

Titles of the Sermon
The Widow's Mite,'
'Adventurous Generosity,'
'Adventurous Faith,'
'Giving All to God.'

Scripture
Luke 21:1-4
Exodus 22:22-24; 23:15; 34:20
Numbers 7:12-18
Deuteronomy 10:18; 16:16; 24:17
I Kings 3:4; 8:63
I Chronicles 29:2-9
Ezra 6:9-17
Isaiah 54:4
Matthew 6:2-4; 23:14
Mark 12:40, 44
Luke 18:1-7; 20:47
II Corinthians 9:6-11

Text: Luke 21:3

A Few Versions of the Text, Luke 21:3

So He said, 'Truly I say to you that this poor widow has put in more than all; *The New King James Version*

And he said, Of a truth I say to you, This poor widow hath cast in more than they all. *Explanatory Notes Upon the New Testament*

And he said, 'Truly I tell you, this poor widow has put in more than all of them; *Revised Standard Version*

"I tell you the truth," he said, "this poor widow has put in more than all the others." *New International Version*

'I tell you this,' he said: 'this poor widow has given more than any of them;' *The New English Bible*

"Really," he remarked, "this poor widow has given more than the rest of them combined." *The Living Bible Illustrated*

He said, "I can guarantee this truth: this poor widow has given more than all the others." *God's Word*

Introduction

The Bible teaches that the believers should serve God in Jesus Christ sacrificially. Christians can serve God with money, talents, and time. There were some Christians who served God most sacrificially. Let us recall a few of those believers.

(1) John Wanamaker (July 11,1838- December 12, 1922) was a U. S. merchant, he founded in 1861 Wanamaker and Brown, a retail clothing store in Philadelphia. He also founded the Bethany Presbyterian Church. He made many contributions to aid benevolent enterprises.[1] He sent a large amount of money to missions in China. He once made a trip to China to see how well the money was used in China. He saw an old man plowing with a crude plowshare which was pulled by an ox and a young man. Mr. Wanamaker asked the old man for an explanation of a strange practice of plowing. The old man told him that his chapel needed spire to be visible for miles around. The members of his church

prayed and denoted some money toward the project but the money was not enough. His son was in the prayer meeting. He suggested his father, "Let us sell one of our oxen and I will take the yoke of the ox as well." When Wanamaker heard this, he said in his prayer, "Lord, let me be hitched to a plow so that I may know the joy of sacrificial giving."[2] The young man gave whatever he could for God's work.

(2) Rev. John Wesley (June 17, 1703-March 2, 1791) gave all for God's work. When he was earning # 30.00 a year, he lived on # 28.00 and gave the remaining #2.00 to the Lord's work. Next year his salary was doubled. He found that he lived comfortably on # 28.00 a year; so instead of rasing his standard of living, he continued to live on #28.00 and gave the whole of his increase to God's work. Because of his sacrificial giving, God entrusted him with large and larger amounts.

In 1787, he told Samuel Bradburn, one of his preachers, that he never gave away anything less than # 1,000.00 a year. From the sale of his books alone, Rev. John Wesley gave away between #30,000.00 and # 40,000.00 When he died, his personal estate amounted to only a few pounds.[3] All these facts point out that Rev. John Wesley gave all to God's work.

(3) General Charles George Gordon (January 28, 1833- January 26, 1885) joined a British force in China in 1860, where he helped to put down the Taiping rebellion.[4] He served faithfully the British Government in China. The Government wanted to reward General Gordon for his magnificent service in China. He declined all money and titles; but he accepted a gold medal on which his thirty-three engagements were inscribed. He was affectionately known as 'Chinese Gordon.'

After his death, the medal could not be found. It was learned that he had sent it to Manchester during a famine, with the request that it be melted and used to buy bread for the famishing poor. The day he sent the medal, he wrote in his diary, "The last and only thing that I had in this world that I valued, I have given over to the Lord Jesus Christ."[5]

General Gordon gave all to God's work.

Introduction of the Text

Why some Christians, like Rev. John Wesley and Chinese Gordon, gave all things to serve God, is explained for the believers in the words of Jesus Christ when He said to His disciples, saying:

> **Truly I tell you, this poor widow has put in more than all of them.**
> (Luke 21:3; Mk 12:43)

This is the text of our meditation now.

The Context of the Text

Jesus Christ went to Jerusalem. He was taken in procession to the temple at Jerusalem, on the first Palm Sunday. He cleansed the temple. He had discussion with the Pharisees and scribes. He was sitting in the part of the temple where thirteen collecting boxes, known as the Trumpets, were placed. People were putting various kinds of offerings for the upkeep of the temple. He saw many people putting their offerings in those boxes. He also saw a poor widow, putting two copper coins in a box. He pointed these facts to His disciples and said to them:

> Truly I tell you, this poor widow has put in more than all of them.
> (Luke 21:3)

This is the text, within its historical background.

An Analysis of the Text

This text has two ideas. (A) The first idea is that the widow had put in the offering box.

(B) The second idea is that Jesus Christ emphatically told His disciples that though her offering was an insignificant amount it was more than the offerings of others.

An Exposition of the Ideas of the Text

(A) The first idea of the text is that the widow had put in the offering box. The widow who put two mites in the temple treasury was poor. That the woman who put her offering was described as widow and poor. These two words described her social and economic condition. The widowhood was not a respectable social condition. Widowhood was considered as a kind of shame and reproach in Israel. Prophet Isaiah referred to the condition of widowhood as follows:

> Fear not, for you will not be ashamed; be not confounded, for you will not be put to shame; for you will forget the shame of your youth, and the reproach of your widowhood you will remember no mere. (Is. 54:4)

As widows had no one to protect them and their belongings, other persons, including religious leaders, were cheating them and grabbing their possessions. Jesus Christ denounced scribes and the Pharisees as they were devouring widows' houses (Lk. 20:47; Mt. 23:14; Mk 12:40).

One can speculate possibilities that the widows, who took their cases to the court, might have been denied justice by judges. Jesus Christ made a parable out of the situation. The parable is called the parable of the unjust judge and a widow (Lk. 18:1-7).

The widows were helpless persons in Israel. The LORD God commanded His people to afford relief to the widows. God commanded thus:

> You shall not afflict any widow or orphan. If you do afflict them, and they cry out to me, I will surely hear their cry; and my wrath will burn, and I will kill you with the sword, and your wives shall become widows and your children fatherless (Ex. 22:22-24 cf. Deut. 24:17).

The LORD God executes justice for the fatherless and the widows (Deut. 10:18).

The widow was poor financially. When her husband died, he did not leave wealth behind him to take care of her. She had no old age pension or other social benefits, during that historical time.

The poor widow went to the temple; and she put two mites in the temple treasury. This shows that she was a religious person. She was obedient to God's command. The LORD God commanded the people of Israel thus: "None shall appear before me empty-handed" (Ex. 23:15; 34:20; Deut. 16:16), when they go for a Passover feast at the temple.

(B) The second idea of the text is that Jesus Christ emphatically told His disciples that though her offering was an insignificant amount it was more than the offerings of others. How can two mites, a penny, could be more than bags of money? How can an insignificant amount of money surpass all other offerings? There must be some spiritual criteria to judge the value of offerings. What were those criteria, which made the poor offering of the widow so rich in the sight of Jesus Christ?

(1) The first criterion is the kind of spirit in which offering is given to God. People offered big gifts to God's work in order to display how rich they were. Such a kind of display gave them social prestige. Jesus was critical of this way of giving gifts to God. He exhorted the people, saying:

> When you give alms, sound no trumpet before you, as the hypocrites do in the synagogues and in the streets, that they may be praised by men. Truly, I say to you, they have received their reward. But when you give alms, do not let your left hand know what your right hand is doing, so that your alms may be in secret; and your Father who sees in secret will reward you. (Mt. 6:2-4)

In other words, a spiritual value of an offering decreases when the offering is made to display or to gain social prestige. On the other hand, the spiritual value of alms-giving increases if it is given in secret.

(2) Secondly, a spiritual value of a gift decreases when it is given unwillingly and with a grudge. St. Paul made this point in his letter to the Corinthians, when he wrote:

> The point is this: he who sows sparingly will also reap sparingly, and he who sows bountifully will also reap bountifully. Each one must do as he has made up his mind, not reluctantly or under compulsion, for God loves a cheerful giver. And God is able to provide you with every blessing in abundance, so that you may always have enough of everything and may provide you in abundance for every good work. As it is written, 'He scatters abroad, he gives

to the poor; his righteousness endures for ever. He who supplies seed to the sower and bread for food will supply and multiply your resources and increase the harvest of your righteousness. You will be enriched in every way for great generosity, which through us will produce thanksgiving to God. (II Cor. 9:6-11)

In other words, a gift, which is given willingly and cheerfully, has more spiritual value than a gift which is given under compulsion or with hesitation.

(3) The third criterion of giving offering is to give gifts with loving hearts. There should be an overflow of love or urge of love to give to God's work. There were many occasions when the people of Israel gave gifts to God's work.

(a) The leaders of twelve tribes of Israel made generous offerings to God's work. (Num. 7:12-18)

(b) King David (1002-962 B. C.) gave all kinds of precious metals to the house of God (I Chr. 29:2-5). Then all leaders of tribes of Israel followed King David (I Chr. 29:6-8). This occasion was concluded with the following remark of the writer of this book, I Chronicles:

Then the people rejoiced because they had given willingly, for with a whole heart they had offered freely to the LORD; David the king also rejoiced greatly. (I Chr. 29:9)

(c) King Solomon (962-922 B. C.) made a thousand burnt offerings upon the altar of God (I Kg. 3:4, cf. I Kg. 8:63).

(d) When the temple at Jerusalem was rebuilt under the leadership of Ezra and Nehemiah, the people generously contributed to God's work. (Ezra 6:9-17)

(4) The fourth and final criterion is to offer oneself to God's work. This principle is stated in the words of Jesus Christ when He explained the significance of the widow's offering, as follows:

for they all contributed out of their abundance, but she out of her poverty put in all the living that she had. (Lk. 21:4)

St. Mark recorded the comment of Jesus Christ in a forceful way, when he wrote these words:

> but she out of her poverty has put in everything she had, her whole living. (Mk 12:44; underline is mine)

In other words, the generosity of the poor widow was more than what was affordable to her. She put everything or her whole living in the temple treasury. It was utterly reckless generosity. She gave all her living to God. That giving must have hurt her. But giving does not begin to be giving until it hurts.

The poor widow did not think about her tomorrow's needs, when she gave all her living to God. She was not anxious about her physical needs on the following days. She gave all to God because she had trust in God's providence. She had an adventurous faith in the divine providence.

Conclusion

The offering of the poor widow to the work of God makes the believers in Jesus Christ to examine their commitment to God's work. They should ask themselves the following questions: Do they give to God's work what is affordable out of their abundance? Do they give their offerings cheerfully? Do they give their offerings willingly? Do they seek public recognition when they give their offerings? Do they serve God with their tithes? Do they serve God by giving more than their tithes? Are they willing to give all as the poor widow did? Do they give priority to serve God over other material concerns? What would Jesus Christ think of their offerings? What can they do to enhance the financial and spiritual condition of their church?

May God grant the Christians the most generous spirit of the poor widow to serve Him with genuine commitment! Amen!

Recommended Hymns from the Methodist Hymnal

182   'When I survey the wondrous Cross'

448   'O Love that wilt not let me go,'

451   'I lift my heart to Thee,'

579   'Saviour, Thy dying love'

595   'God of almighty love,'

Recommended Responsive Reading from the Methodist Hymnal

30 (p. 396).

Recommended Responsive Reading from *A Worship Manual for Scriptural or Methodist Order of Service*

23 (p. 108-109).

Endnotes

[1] The New American Encyclopedia, Vol. 20, p. 7194.

[2] Paul Lee Tan, Encyclopedia of 7700 Illustrations: Signs of the Times, # 1826.

[3] *Ibid.,* # 1828.

[4] The New American Encyclopedia, Vol. 9, pp. 3384f.

[5] *Ibid.,* # 1830.

Chapter 11

Titles of the Sermon

'Abundant Receiving and Generous or Graceful Giving,'

'Conditional Divine Blessings,'

'Abundance for Oneself and for Good Work,'

'Providential Abundance for Every Good Work.'

Scripture

II Corinthians 9:1-15

Genesis 4:6-8; 12:1-3; 13:2; 14:14, 20

Exodus 12:40; 23:16-17

Leviticus 27:30, 32

Deuteronomy 7:6-11; 8:3-4; 15:7-11; 16:16-17; 25:5-6;
26:12-13; 28:22

I Kings 17:8-16

I Chronicles 28:2-6, 12-18: 29:7-8, 10-13

Psalms 23:1; 34:9-10; 37:25-26; 84:11

Proverbs 14:31; 19:17

Malachi 3:6-12

Matthew 7:2; 25:34-40

Philippians 4:19

Hebrews 11:4

James 1:27

I John 3:12-13

Text: II Corinthians 9:8

A Few Versions of the Text, II Corinthians 9:8

And God is able to make all grace abound towards you, that you, always having all sufficiency in all things, may have an abundance for every good work. *The New King James Version*

And God is able to make all grace abound towards ye; that having always all sufficiency in all things, ye may abound to every good work; *Explanatory Notes Upon the New Testament*

And God is able to provide you with every blessing in abundance, so that you may always have enough of everything and may provide in abundance for every good work. *Revised Standard Version*

And God is able to make all grace abound towards you, so that in all things at all times, having all that you need, you will abound in every good work. *New International Version*

And it is in God's power to provide you richly with every good gift; thus you will have ample means in yourselves to meet each and every situation, with enough and to spare for every good cause. *The New English Bible*

And God is able to make it up to you by giving you everything you need and more, so that there will not only be enough for your own needs, but plenty left over to give joyfully to others. *The Living Bible Illustrated*

Besides, God will give you his constantly overflowing kindness. Then, when you always have everything you need, you can do more and more good things. *God's Word*

Introduction

There are many illustrations in the Bible to tell us how man responded to God's gracious and abundant care and provision.

(1) Adam had two sons- Cain and Abel. Cain was a farmer and Abel, a shepherd. They brought offerings to the LORD God. Cain brought the fruit of the ground; and Abel brought firstlings of his flock and their fat portions. For a reason, God had regard for Abel

and his offering; but God had no regard for Cain and his offering. Therefore Cain was very angry and his countenance fell. Then God said to Cain:

Why are you angry, and why has your countenance fallen? If you do well, will you not be accepted? And if you do not do well, sin is couching at your door; its desire is for you, but you must master it. (Gen. 4:6-7)

The reason, why God had no regard for Cain and his offering, is implied in the story that God knew that Cain had no right spirit in offering the gifts to God; and he had no right relationship with his brother, Abel. The heart of Cain was filled with evil spirit, envy and malice (I Jn 3:12-13); therefore, he killed his brother, Abel (Gen. 4:8). The LORD God had regard for Abel and his offerings, because Abel offered the gifts to God in faith (Heb. 11:4). This event teaches the believers that they have to appreciate God's gracious and abundant provision by giving gifts to God with sincere hearts.

(2) David was a shepherd; but God made him a powerful king of the people of Israel. King David (1002-962 B. C.) always remembered what God did for him; therefore, he had an intention to build the first temple for the LORD God. He asked officials of Israel, officials of the tribes, commanders of his army, and other mighty men to gather together. Whey they assembled together, King David said to them:

Hear me, my brethren and my people, I had it in my heart to build a house of rest for the ark of the covenant of the LORD, and for the foot stool of our God; and I made preparation for building. But God said to me, 'you may not build a house for my name, for you are a warrior and have shed blood... he [the LORD] has chosen Solomon my son to sit upon the throne of the kingdom of the LORD over Israel. He said to me, 'It is Solomon your son who shall build my house and my courts, for I have chosen him to be my son, and I will be his father. (I Chr. 28:2-6)

Then King David gave Solomon a plan for the vestibule of the temple, its houses, inner chambers, the room for a mercy seat, the courts of the house of God, all the surrounding chambers. He gave gold, silver, and other things for the vessels, and costumes for the service in the temple. (I Chr. 28:12-18) Then he gave from his private possession

3,000 talents of gold and 7,000 talents of silver. Then other people made contributions toward building the first temple of God. (I Chr. 29:7-8)

Then King David blessed the LORD God, in the presence of the great assembly, saying:

> Blessed art thou, O LORD, the God of Israel our father, for ever and ever. Thine, O LORD, is the greatness, the victory, and the majesty; for all that is in heaven and in the earth is thine; thine is the kingdom, O LORD, and thou art exalted as head above all.... ...Both riches and honour come from thee, and thou rulest over all. In thy hand are power and might; and in thy hand it is to make great and give strength to all. And now we thank thee, our God, and praise thy glorious name. (I Chr. 29:10-13)

King David and the leaders of Israel acknowledged what God had done for them; they expressed their gratitude by generous donations for the work of God.

Introduction of the Text

The spiritual tradition of acknowledging God's provision, and thanking God by generous gifts to His work had been upheld by the Church, which is God's new Israel. St. Paul introduced this old practice of Judaism to the newly established churches; and he exhorted Christians to give to God's work. He wrote to Christians at Corinth:

> **God is able to provide you with every blessing in abundance, so that you have enough of everything and may provide in abundance for every good work.** (II Corinthians 9:8)

This is the text of our meditation now.

The Context of the Text

St. Paul was raising funds for the mother church at Jerusalem. Christians at Corinth were taught to be generous to others. They were practising this virtue always. They had sent help to the mother church at Jerusalem many times. But there was a special need to raise funds for the mother church. When St. Paul mentioned the special need of the church at Jerusalem, the church at Corinth promised to send a gift. He told them that he praised them for their generosity to the people at

Macedonia. In his reminder to them, he wrote that it was superfluous for him to remind them to send the gift to the church at Jerusalem, as they promised. He was very sure of their generosity. On the basis of the scripture, he exhorted them, saying:

> God is able to provide you with every blessing in abundance, so that you have enough of everything and may provide in abundance for every good work. (II Corinthians 9:8)

This is the text, within its historical background.

An Analysis of the Text

This text has four ideas. (A) The first idea is that God is able to provide the believers with every blessing.

(B) The second idea is that God provides His people in abundance.

(C) The third idea is that the first purpose of the abundant provision, which is, that God's people may have enough of every thing.

(D) The fourth idea is the second purpose of the abundant provision, which is, that God's people be able to do every good work.

Exposition of the Ideas of the Text

(A) The first idea of the text is that God is able to provide the believers with every blessing. God is the provider of His people. He, therefore, is called 'Jehovah Jireh," in Hebrew language. He provides every need of His people, who believe in Him. God keeps His promises and covenants, which He made with His servants. One of the servants of God was Abraham. Abraham is the spiritual father of the faith and of the commitment of the people to God. God said to Abraham:

> Go from your country and your kindred and your father's house to the land that I will show you. And I will make of you a great nation, and I will bless you, and make your name great, so that you will be a blessing. I will bless those who bless you, and him who curses you I will curse; and by you all the families of the earth shall bless themselves. (Gen. 12:1-3)

Abraham trusted in God's promise; and he, in faith in God, migrated from Ur of Chaldeans to Canaan, the promised land. Out of Abraham, God created a great nation of Israel.

The people of Israel were in the bondage of Egypt for four hundred and thirty years (Ex. 12:40). God, through Moses, brought them out of the bondage. Those liberated people started their journey through the wilderness to the promised land. In the wilderness, there was no fertile land to cultivate food; there were no rivers of water to drink from; there were no industry to provide clothes. In the wilderness, God. gave them manna, as daily food; He gave them water to drink; and He provided enough clothing and shoes for forty years (Deut. 8:3-4).

Moses experienced how God supplied the needs of His people. He saw that God's provisions for his people was conditional; and he knew why God chose the people of Israel. He said to the people of Israel:

> For you are a people holy to the LORD your God; the Lord your God has chosen you to be a people for his own possession, out of all the peoples that are on the face of earth. It was not because you were more in number than any other people that the LORD set his love upon you and chose you, for you were the fewest of all people; but it is because the LORD loves you, and is keeping the oath which he swore to your fathers, that the LORD has brought you out with a mighty hand, and redeemed your from the house of bondage, from the hand of Pharaoh king of Egypt. Know therefore that the LORD your God is God, the faithful God who keeps covenant and steadfast love with those who love him and keep his commandments, to a thousand generations, and requite to their face those who hate him, by destroying them,.... You shall therefore be careful to do the commandments, and statutes, and the ordinances, which I command you this day. (Deut. 7:6-11)

This scriptural passage confirms that God is the provider of the people, who would obey His commands. And His provision is conditional, in terms of keeping His statutes, ordinances, and commandments.

(B) The second idea of the text is that God provides His people in abundance. His provision in abundance is conditional. God gave some commandments to His people that they may obey them. One of the divine commandments was to serve God with tithes. There are some examples to substantiate this idea.

(1) Abraham was very rich, owning innumerable flocks, herds, and many servants. (Gen. 13:2; 14:14) God made Abraham very rich, because Abraham was His faithful servant, keeping God's commandments. The scripture tells us that Abraham once gave tithes to Melchizedek, who was a high priest of God. (Gen. 14:20)

(2) Isaac inherited all wealth from his father Abraham. (Gen. 25:5, 6) Isaac learned from his father the practice of giving tithes to God. Isaac taught this practice to his son Jacob, who gave tithes of all things to God. (Gen. 28:22) It is needless to tell that God's servants gave their tithes for God's work.; they had faithfully maintained this spiritual tradition from generation to generation.

(3) Moses was a faithful servant of the LORD God. Through Moses, God commanded the people of Israel to give tithes of all things. Moses said the people of Israel:

> All the tithes of the land, whether of the seed of the land or the fruit of the trees, is the LORD's; it is holy to the LORD... And all the tithes of herds and flocks, every tenth animal of all that pass under herdsman's staff, shall be holy to the LORD. (Lev. 27:30, 32)

All people of Israel were expected to give tithes of everything to God. They were asked to bring their offerings at the time of various feasts, which were celebrated at the temple. As God was blessing everyone, no one was expected to enter the temple of God empty-handed. God said to the people of Israel:

> No one shall come into my presence empty-handed. You shall celebrate the pilgrim-feast of Harvest, with the first-fruits of your work in sowing the land, and the pilgrim feast of Ingathering at the end of the year, when you bring in fruits of all your work on the land. (Ex. 23:16-17)

This divine law was to be maintained by every person in all conditions, even in difficult situations. Man was to give priority to supporting God's work. When a person obeys God and gives priority to God's work, he or she is blessed by God abundantly. This truth was reaffirmed by an historical event, as follows.

Once there was drought and famine in the land of Israel. God asked prophet Elijah to go to Zarephath. When prophet Elijah approached the city, he saw a widow gathering sticks. He approached her and said to her, "Bring me a little water in a vessel, that I may drink."(I Kg. 17:10) Then he added, "Bring me a morsel of bread in your hand." (I Kg. 17:11) The widow replied to prophet Elijah, saying:

> I have only a handful of meal in a jar, and a little oil in a cruse; and now I am gathering a couple of sticks, that I may go in and prepare it for myself and my son, that we may eat it and die. (I Kg. 17:12)

Then prophet Elijah said to the widow:

> Fear not; go and do as you have said; but first make a little cake of it and bring it to me, and afterward make for yourself and your son. For thus says the LORD God of Israel, 'The jar of meal shall not be spent, and the cruse of oil shall not fail, until the day that the LORD sends rain upon the earth. (I Kg. 17:13-15)

The widow believed in prophet Elijah and in the promise of the LORD God. She did as prophet Elijah instructed her. She did not doubt the words of prophet Elijah and the promise of God. Therefore, the supply of oil and meal remained constant. The supply was a great deal for her family all the time; and she was able to take care of God's servant. If the widow had not believed in the promise of God, and if she had not first brought a small cake for God's man; and ate all she had, she and her son would have died of starvation for the days until their deaths. But in the face of a critical situation, she believed in the promise of God and obeyed what the servant of God had said; therefore, she was able to see the mysterious supply of the oil and meal at all times.

God gives to His faithful servants all things in abundance. King David (1002-962 B. C.), in a famous psalm, stated his spiritual experience in these words, "The LORD is my shepherd, I shall not want." (Ps. 23:1) He again said in another psalm, "They that shall seek the LORD shall not want any good thing. " (Ps. 34: 9f.) Another psalm writer endorsed this experience in these words, "No good thing does the LORD withhold from those who walk uprightly." (Ps. 84:11)

The LORD God was manifested in Jesus Christ. St. Paul experienced God's care for him. He, therefore, was able to give the divine assurance to Christians when he wrote these words:

My God shall supply all your needs, according to His riches in glory by Jesus Christ. (Phil. 4:19)

God satisfies all needs of His people in abundance, when the people keep His commandments. But, on the other hand, when the people disobey God and they do not give tithes to God's work, God withholds His blessings, and He causes shortage of every good thing. Concerning this spiritual fact, God said to the people of Israel, through prophet Malachi, the following words:

From the days of you fathers you have turned aside from my statutes and have not kept them. Return to me, and I will return to you, says the LORD of host. But you say, 'How shall we return? Will man rob God? Yet you are robbing me. But you say, 'How are we robbing thee?' In your tithes and offerings. You are cursed with a curse, for you are robbing me, the whole nation of you. Bring the full tithes into the storehouse, that there may be food in my house; and thereby put me to the test, says the LORD of hosts, if I will not open the windows of heaven for you and pour down for you an overflowing blessing. I will rebuke the devourer for you, so that it will not destroy the fruits of your soil; and your vine in the field shall not fail to bear... Then all nations call you blessed, for you will be a land of delight, says the LORD of hosts. (Mal. 3:6-12)

(C) The third idea of the test is the first purpose of the abundant provision, which is, that God's people may have enough of every thing. This divine provision is made also for an individual believer. King David experienced this divine blessing in his life. Out of his experience, he said:

O Fear the LORD, ye his servants; for there is no want to them that fear him. The young lions do lack and suffer hunger; but they that seek the LORD shall not want any good thing. (Ps. 34:9-10)

King David bore the witness to God's constant provision to His servants, when he said:

I have been young and now am old; yet I have not seen the righteous forsaken or his children begging bread. He is ever giving and lending, and his children become a blessing. (Ps. 37:25-26)

A righteous person, who keeps God's laws, including the giving tithes of everything to God, is blessed by God always. It means that there is a definite relationship between man's giving to God and God's blessings to man. Man is expected to give to God's work in accordance with the blessings of the LORD God. (Deut. 16:16-17) The more man gives to God's work, the more he receives God's blessing. On the basis of this spiritual fact, St. Paul wrote to the Corinthians:

> The point is this: he who sows sparingly will also reap sparingly, and he who sows bountifully will also reap bountifully. (II Cor. 9:6)

This spiritual law states that one will be rewarded in proportion to one's giving. This truth was stated by Jesus Christ Himself, in the following words, "The measure you give will be measure you get." (Mt. 7:2) God gives all things to His faithful servants enough to satisfy their needs. This is the first purpose why God gives enough of every thing to His servants.

(D) The fourth idea of the text is the second purpose of the abundant provision, which is, that God's people be able to do every good work. The Bible defines good works as charitable deeds, which are done to relieve the needy from their plight, such as, helping widows, orphans, helpless, and the poor. The gifts, which were given by God, were to be used for these charitable deeds.

Every third year was to be observed as paying all the tithes to God. The people of Israel were commanded to give tithes towards the needy and helpless. This was a divine law to serve the charitable purposes. God inspired Moses to write the law, as follows:

> When you have finished paying all the tithes of your produce in the third year, which is the year of tithing, giving it to the Levite, the sojourner, the fatherless, and the widow, that they may eat within your towns and be filled, then you shall say before the LORD your God, 'I have removed the sacred portions out of my house, and moreover I have given it to the Levite, the sojourner, the fatherless, and the widow, according to all thy commandment which thou hast commanded me; I have not transgressed any of thy commandments, neither have I forgotten them; (Deut. 26:12-13)

God has commanded to His people to be charitable to the poor and the needy; He ordered a provision for them. It is a sin not to help the poor and the needy. The LORD God said the following words to His people:

If there is among you a poor man, one of your brethren, in any of your towns within your land which the LORD your God gives you, and you shall not harden your heart or shut your hand against your poor brother, but you shall open your hand to him, and lend him sufficient for his need, whatever it may be. Take heed lest there be a base thought in your heart, and you say, 'The seventh year, the year of release is near,' and your eye be hostile to your poor brother, and you give him nothing, and he cry to the LORD against you, and it be a sin in you. You shall give him freely, and your heart shall not be grudging when you give him; because of this the LORD will bless you in all your work and in all that you undertake. For the poor will never cease out of the land; therefore I command you, You shall open wide your hand to your brother, to the needy and to the poor, in the land. (Deut. 15:7-11)

King Solomon, in two proverbs, summarized the thought as follows:

he who oppresses a poor man insults his Maker, but he who is kind to the needy honours him. (Pr. 14:31)

And,

He who is kind to the poor lends to the LORD, and he will repay him for his deed. (Pr. 19:17)

Jesus Christ, in the parable of sheep and goats, reiterated the teaching, in these words:

Then the King will say to those at his right hand, 'Come, O blessed of my Father, inherit the kingdom prepared for you from the foundation of the world; for I was hungry and you gave me food, and I was thirsty and you gave me drink, and I was a stranger and you welcomed me, I was naked and you clothed me, I was sick and you visited me, I was in prison and you came to me.' Then the righteous will answer him, 'Lord, when did you we see thee hungry and feed thee, or thirsty and give you drink? And when did we see thee sick or in prison and visit thee? And the King will answer them, 'Truly, I say to you, as you did it to one of the least of these my brethren, you did it to me. (Mt. 25:34-40)

Apostles of Jesus Christ continued this teaching in churches. St. James defined a true religion in these words:

Religion that is pure and undefiled before God and the Father is this: to visit orphans and widows in their affliction, and to keep oneself unstained from the world. (Jas. 1:27)

God provides His people abundantly so that they would be charitable to the poor and the needy. This is the second purpose of God's abundant provision for His people. Caring for others and especially for the poor, widows, orphans, and strangers is to practise love of God in daily life. St. Paul asked the Corinthians to send help to the poor saints at Jerusalem, because he knew the second purpose of God's abundant provision to the believers in Jesus Christ.

Conclusion

God is the provider of the people, who obey His commandments. His provision is conditional. He commanded His people to serve Him with their tithes of everything; and He promised them that they would have everything in abundance always for themselves; they would not lack any good thing. God's people were asked to share their blessings with the poor, needy, widows, orphans, and strangers. They were expected to do every charitable work out of the abundance they have received from God. St. Paul exhorted Christians to do the charitable works, because God had blessed them abundantly. Doing charitable deeds to others is to lend to the Lord Jesus Christ. He would bless His people abundantly that they may not lack anything; and they give in charity. Giving to the needy is a way of sincerely thanking God for His blessings.

Recommended Hymns from the Methodist Hymnal

10   'Now thank we all our God,'

76   'The King of my love my Shepherd is,'

427   'Through all the changing'

550   'O For a heart to praise my God,'

567   'In full and glad surrender'

672   'Saviour, blessed Saviour,'

851   'All things bright and beautiful,'

962   'Come, ye faithful people, come,'

963   'We plough the fields, and scatter'

968   'Yes, God is good - in earth and sky,'

969   'O Lord of heaven and earth and sea,'

Recommended Responsive Reading from the Methodist Hymnal

\# 29 (p. 395) or,

\# 51 (p. 406) or,

\# 61(p. 411),

Recommended Responsive Reading from A Worship Manual for Scriptural or Methodist Order of Service

\# 22 (pp. 106-108) or,

\# 98 (pp.230-231) or,

\# 59 (pp. 161-163).

Part II
Two Textual Sermons on Anniversary Day

Chapter 12

Titles of the Sermon:

'A Divine Determination

'Different, therefore, Successful,'

'Vision, Venture, and Victory.'

Scripture

Numbers 13:17-14:10

Genesis 12:1, 7; 15:7, 13, 18; 17:7-8

Exodus 7:9-12, 19-20; 8:6, 17; 9:23-24; 10:13-15; 11:4-5;12:40-41; 14:13, 21, 27-28.

Numbers 10:11; 13:2; 32:8-13; 14:28-34

Deuteronomy 1:19-46

Joshua 14:13-14

I Samuel 17:34-37, 47

II Chronicles 20:1-12, 15-17, 22-24

Psalms 20:7-8; 46:1-3

Matthew 8:3; 20:34

Mark 1:42; 2:12

Luke 5:25; 8:43-44; 18:43

John 5:9

Text: Numbers 13:30

A Few Versions of the Text, Numbers 13:30:

'Let us go up at once and take possession, for we are able to overcome it.' *New King James Version*

Let us go up at once, and possess it; for we are well able to overcome it. *The Wesleyan Bible Commentary*

'Let us go up at once, and occupy it; for we are well able to overcome it.' *Revised Standard Version*

'We should go up and take possession of the land, for we can certainly do it.' *New International Version*

'Let us go up at once and occupy the country; we are well able to conquer it.' *The New English Bible*

'Let us go up at once and possess it,' he said, 'for we are well able to conquer it! ' *The Living Bible Illustrated*

'Let's go now and take possession of the land. We should be more than able to conquer it.' *God's Word*

Introduction

(1) In Canada we had Woolworth stores. Mr. Frank Winfield Woolworth (April 13, 1852 – April 8, 1919) was their founder. He was a merchant from New York city. He came with an idea of stores selling items at the price of five and ten cents, when other merchants were selling items at higher prices. Woolworth's idea was different from others.

When he passed away, his fortune was measured in millions, it amounted to$65 millions. He was different, therefore, he was successful.

(2) Mr. Henry Ford (July 30, 1863 – April 7, 19467), the founder of Ford Automaker Company, came with an idea to build a light, cheap car for millions. His idea was different from others, when other were producing cars for the rich at higher prices. His cars became popular. Ford Company has branches throughout the world. He was different; therefore, he was successful.

(3) Mr. John Wanamaker (July 11, 1838 – December 12, 1922) conceived an idea of one-price to every thing in his retail stores. His policy was different from the accepted practice throughout the country, i.e., different prices for different things. He was successful as Mr. Woolworth and Mr. Ford.

These illustrations convey an idea that progress has often depended on the courage of man, who dared to be different. You need to be different in order to make a difference in society.

Introduction of the Text

Really godly persons or leaders are peculiar or strange persons from other people. They dare to be different; therefore, they can lead to victory. Caleb was one of those leaders. He said to the people of Israel when they were frightened by others:

> **Let us go up at once, and occupy it; for we are well able to overcome it.** (Numbers 13:30)

The Context of the Text

The LORD God said to Abram, "Go from your country and your kindred and your father's house to the land that I will show you." (Gen. 12:1) Abram did not know where that land was; but he believed in the promise of God, and he continued his journey toward the land. While he was passing through Canaan, the LORD God appeared to Abram and said to him, "To your descendants I will give this land." (Gen. 12:7 cf. Gen. 15:7, 18) God made a covenant with Abram as follows:

> I will establish my covenant between me and you and your descendants after you throughout their generations for an everlasting covenant, to be God to you and to your descendants after you. And I will give to you, and to your descendants after you, the land of your sojourning, all the land of Canaan, for an everlasting possession; and I will be their God. (Gen. 17:7-8)

Abraham saw the promised land. He believed that God would give the land to his descendants. His descendants, the people of Israel, were in slavery of Pharaoh of Egypt for more than four hundred years

(Gen. 15:13; Ex. 12:40-41). God raised Moses to be the leader of Israelites; and Moses liberated them from Egyptian bondage. Moses was leading his people to the promised land.

The people of Israel travelled through the wilderness for more than a year. When they approached the promised land in the second year (Num. 10:11), and when the people of Israel were at Kadeshbarnea (Deut. 1:19), God asked Moses to send twelve leaders to spy the land, saying:

> Send men to spy out the land of Canaan, which I give to the people of Israel; from each tribe of their fathers shall you send a man, every one a leader among them. (Num. 13:2)

The twelve leaders spied the land for forty days (Num. 13:25). They went back to Moses, Aaron, and the people of Israel, with fruit from the Valley of Eschol (Deut. 1:24-25; Num. 13:23; 32:9). They told the people of Israel that the land flowed with milk and honey; and it had plenty of fruit (Num. 13:27). However, the ten leaders told the people of Israel that the people who dwelt in the land were strong, and of great stature; they were the descendants of Anak; we seemed to ourselves as grasshoppers before Nephilim (the sons of Anak) (Num. 13:28, 33). The cities of the dwellers were fortified and strong (Num. 13:28). They also told the people of Israel that the land devoured its people (Num. 13:32). This report terrified the people of Israel. They told Moses, Aaron, and the people of Israel:

> We are not able to go up against the people; for they are stronger than we. The land devours its inhabitants; and all the people that we saw in it are men of great stature... we seemed to ourselves like grasshoppers, and so we seemed to them. (Num. 13:31-33).

Those ten leaders advised the people of Israel against the advice of Caleb, who had said early to them:

> Let us go up at once, and occupy it; for we are well able to overcome it. (Num. 13:30)

The people of Israel were frightened of being killed by the inhabitants; therefore, they were thinking to go back to Egypt (Num. 14:4). To these frightened people, Joshua and Caleb said:

> The land, which we passed through to spy it out, is an exceedingly good land. If the LORD delights in us, he will bring us into this land and give it to us, a land which flows with milk and honey. Only, do not rebel against the LORD; and do not fear the people of the land; for they are bread for us; their protection is removed from them, and the LORD is with us; do not fear them. (Num. 14:9)

When the people heard these words, they began to stone Caleb and Joshua. God was angry with the people. He told Moses that none of those, who despised God, would enter the land, except Caleb and his descendants, who would enter the land and possess it.

An Analysis of the Text

The text of our meditation is: "Let us go up at once, and occupy it; for we are well able to overcome it." (Numbers 13:30) This text has two ideas.

(A) The first idea is that Caleb told the people of Israel to act immediately and possess the land.

(B) The second idea is that Caleb told the people of Israel that they were well able to overcome the land.

An Exposition of the Ideas

(A) The first idea of the text is that Caleb told the people of Israel to act immediately and possess the land.

What were the reasons of the advice of Caleb to the people of Israel, which was against the position of other ten leaders?

By upholding the different perspective on the terrifying situation, Caleb proved himself to be different from other ten leaders. Caleb had full trust in the promise and power of God. He showed his wholehearted faith in God.

Caleb was one of those leaders, who were chosen to spy the promised the land, during the second year after the exodus from Egypt and crossing the Red Sea. Caleb was an eyewitness of all the miracles, which Moses and Aaron performed in Egypt in order to compel Pharaoh to let the people of Israel go out of his land. Those miracles or the plagues were the divine or supernatural actions. They were performed instantly.

When Moses asked Aaron to cast the rod on the floor in the presence of Pharaoh, the rod immediately turned into a serpent, which swallowed other serpents, made by magicians of Egypt (Ex. 7:9-12). When Aaron, at the command of Moses, stretched the rod on waters of Egypt and on the Nile, all water turned into blood immediately (Ex. 7:19-20). When Aaron, at the command of Moses, stretched his hand with the rod on the water of Egypt, frogs came up from water and covered Egypt (Ex. 8:6). In a similar way, when Aaron struck the dust of the earth, it became gnats throughout Egypt (Ex. 8:17).

When Moses stretched forth his rod toward heaven, the LORD God sent thunder, hail, and fire (Ex. 9:23-24). When Moses stretched forth his rod over the land of Egypt, the locusts came and devoured every plant (Ex. 10:13-15). God told to Moses the final plague that He would bring upon Egyptians. God killed the firstborn of Egyptians and of cattle (Ex. 11:4-5). After this miracle, Pharaoh allowed the people of Israel to leave Egypt, with all their possessions.

When the people of Israel encamped by the sea, Pharaoh sent his army to capture them. The people of Israel were afraid, when they saw Pharaoh's chariots. Moses told them not to fear, but to see the salvation of the LORD (Ex. 14:13). At the command of the LORD God, Moses stretched forth his hand on the sea; and the sea was divided. People of Israel went in the midst of the sea, on dry land (Ex. 14:21). When the people of Israel passed through the sea, God asked Moses to stretch forth his hand on the sea, the water returned and covered the Egyptians (Ex. 14:27-28).

Caleb saw all these miracles. He was convinced that God redeemed the people of Israel through His mighty deeds. Moreover, God performed those miracles instantly. Caleb understood that God kept His promise to redeem Israel from slavery by doing mighty acts instantly. Therefore, Caleb believed that God would keep His promise to give the promised land to His people. Caleb never doubted God's promise and His power to fulfill His promise. This was the main reason why he advised the people of Israel "Let us go up at once, and occupy it." (Num. 13:30)

In his exhortation to the people of Israel, he said to them that they should not be afraid of the inhabitants of land, because God had removed their protection; therefore, they would be like a bread to them. Moreover, the LORD God was with them and they should not rebel against Him (Num. 14:9). In other words, he assured them of an instant victory on the inhabitants of land, because God wanted to keep His promise to give the land to them, and He would work miracles to fulfil His promise; but the people of Israel had to be obedient to the LORD God.

The majority of the people of Israel, represented by the ten leaders, did not act on the advice of Caleb and Joshua. They were afraid of the stronger inhabitants of the land. They questioned God's promise. Therefore, God was angry at them. God told Moses that those people, who disobeyed Him, would not enter the promised land, except Caleb and his descendants. Those disobedient people would wander forty years in the wilderness and die in their journey (Num. 14:29-34).

There are some examples in the New Testament to confirm that God in Jesus Christ acted instantly. When Jesus stretched his hand and touched a leper, his leprosy was cleansed immediately (Mt. 8:3; Mk. 1:42). When Jesus touched the eyes of two blind men, they received their sight immediately (Mt. 20:34; Lk. 18:43). Jesus healed the paralytic immediately (Mk. 2:12; Lk. 5:25; Jn 5:9). When a woman, who had a flow of blood for twelve years, touched the fringe of Jesus' garment, she was healed immediately (Lk. 8:43-44).

(B) The second idea of the text is that Caleb told the people of Israel that they were well able to overcome the land. He told them that they would defeat the mighty inhabitants, because God was with them, and He had removed the protection from the inhabitants. He was not afraid of the inhabitants, though they were physically stronger than the people of Israel, and their cities were fortified. His confidence was not in human strength but it was in the power of God.

Caleb believed that God would act instantly and He would not delay keeping His promise. He had "wholehearted faith" in God (Deut. 1:36). He was ready to demonstrate the essence of his true faith in God, in the face of adversaries.

Caleb's "wholehearted faith" became an example for those who act on faith in God, in the face of adversaries; he demonstrated the essence of the true faith in God. His firm faith is an example for all generations.[1] Because of his firm faith in God, God honoured the faith of Caleb by giving him Hebron as his inheritance (Jos. 14:13-14).

Like Caleb, David had faith in God's protection, in the face of adversaries. The Philistines and army of King Saul (ca 1082-1042 B. C.) were about to fight at Socoh. A champion of the Philistines, named Goliath, challenged the army of Saul, saying them to send their warrior to fight against him (I Sam. 17:10). When King Saul and all Israel heard these words of Goliath, they were greatly afraid (I Sam. 17:24).

Jesse, of Bethlem, sent his youngest son David to take food for his three brothers, who were on the battle field. David saw Goliath and heard Goliath's challenge; and saw how the army of King Saul was afraid. David wanted to accept the challenge of Goliath. King Saul called David and David said to King Saul that he would fight against the Philistine. King Saul said to David that he was young and without experience of a warrior. Then David told King Saul, how he was engaged in fights against beasts and how God delivered him from those fights thus:

> Your servant used to keep sheep for his father; and when there came a lion, or a bear, and took a lamb from the flock, I went after him and smote him and delivered it out of his mouth; and if he arose against me, I caught him by his beard, and smote him and killed him. Your servant has killed both lions and bears; and this uncircumcised Philistine shall be one of them, seeing he has defied the armies of the living God.... The Lord who delivered me from the paw of the lion and from the paw of the bear, will deliver me from the hand of this Philistine. (I Sam. 17:34-37)

David experienced God's protection on many occasions; therefore, he built his belief that God would continue to protect him in the face of adversaries. David had trust in God and not in his own strength. He was not afraid of the stature of Goliath and his big sword and spear, as other warriors of King Saul were afraid. David's confidence was not in human strength and in weapons, but it was in God. David said to Goliath, testifying God's power, in these words:

> You come to me with a sword and with a spear and with a javelin; but I come to you in the name of the LORD of host, the God of the armies of Israel, whom you have defied... and that all this assembly may know that the LORD saves not with sword and spear; for the battle is the LORD's and he will give you in our hands. (I Sam. 17:45, 47)

David went in the name of God to fight against the most fearful warrior. He had a different outlook of the battle. He killed Goliath and won victory over the Philistines. David had a vision; he ventured to fight against the enemy; and he had victory. In a psalm King David (1002-962 B. C.) wrote:

> Some boast of chariots, and some of horses; but we boast of the name of the LORD our God. They will collapse and fall; but we shall rise and stand upright. (Ps. 20:7-8)

When the men of Moab, Amon, and Mount Seir set ambush against Jerusalem and Judah, King Jehoshaphat (873-849 B. C.) of Judah was afraid of those people. He asked the people of Judah to seek God's help. They fasted and prayed to the LORD God for protection (II Chr. 20:1-12). Jahaziel spoke to the assembly in the name of God:

> Hearken, all Judah and inhabitants of Jerusalem and King Jehoshaphat: Thus says the LORD to you, 'Fear not, and be not dismayed at this great multitude; for the battle is not yours but God's. Tomorrow go down against them; behold, they will come up by the ascent of Ziz; you will find them at the end of the valley, east of the wilderness of Jeruel. You will not need to fight in the battle; take your position, stand still, and see the victory of the LORD on your behalf, O Judah and Jerusalem.' Fear not, and be not dismayed; tomorrow go out against them, and the LORD will be with you. (II Chr. 20:15-17)

The people obeyed the command of the LORD God; and they marched against their enemies. The men of Moab and Ammon rose against the men of Mount Seir; and they killed them, and then they helped to destroy one another. God gave the victory to the people of Judah over their enemies (II Chr. 20:22-24).

A psalm writer expressed his confidence in God's protection when he wrote these words:

> God is our refuge and strength, a very present help in trouble. Therefore we will not fear though the earth should change, though the mountains shake in the heart of the sea; though its waters roar and foam, though the mountains tremble with its tumult. (Ps. 46:1-3)

Conclusion

Caleb said to the people of Israel, 'Let us go up at once, and occupy it; for we are well able to overcome it.' (Num. 13:30) By saying so, he expressed his faith in God. Mr. William Stoughton (A. D.1630-1701) said about faith, "Faith does nothing alone, nothing of itself, but everything under God, by God, and through God."[2] Caleb's faith was God-centred. Mr. George W. Ridout (1871-1880), the Wesleyan Methodist, said, "Faith will begat in us three things: Vision, Venture, Victory."[3] These three Vs were to be found in Caleb, when he said the words of our text. Rev. Charles Wesley, a founder of Methodism, was like Caleb, believing God would make impossible things possible through him. He wrote:

> 'Twas most impossible of all
>
> That here sin's reign in me should cease.
>
> Yet shall it be, I know it shall;
>
> Jesus look to Thy faithfulness!
>
> If nothing is too hard for Thee,
>
> All things are possible to me."[4]

Caleb's faith in God was to teach the believers that "With God all things are possible" (Mt. 19:26, Mk 10:27) and "all things are possible to him that believes" (Mk. 9:23). When the believers have firm faith, they would have visions, they would venture in the name of God, and they would be victorious. Let us be like Caleb and have these three Vs in us in order to serve God in obedience to Him.

Conclusion

We are celebrating our twenty-fifth church anniversary today. On this day, we should recall how God miraculously helped us in the past years. As Caleb recalled the events of redemption in the life of his people Israel, we similarly recall the redemptive events in the life of the congregation. Caleb had perspective of three Vs, namely, vision, venture, and victory in his committed life to God. We should have these three Vs in our individual and collective life in order to make our life progressive and prosperous. May God in Jesus Christ bless us with this positive perspective about God's work in us and through us. Amen.

Recommended Hymns from the Methodist Hymnal

238   'My faith looks up to Thee,'

485   'I'm not ashamed to own my Lord,'

488   'Oft in danger; oft in woe,'

490   'Fight the good fight with all thy might;'

        verse 24 (p. 380)

Recommended Responsive Reading from the Methodist Hymnal

27 (p. 394),

Recommended Responsive Reading from *A Worship Manual for Scriptural or Methodist Order of Service*

20 (pp. 103-104).

Endnotes

[1] Paul D. Gardener, editor, The Complete Who's Who in the Bible, (Grand Rapids, Michigan: Zondervan Publishing House, 1995), p. 96.

[2] Frank S. Mead (ed.) The Encyclopedia of Religious Quotations, (Old Tappan, New Jersey: Fleming H. Revell Co., 1965), p. 137.

[3] *Ibid.*, p. 137.

[4] Duncan Campbell, God's Answer: Revival Sermons, (Edinburgh: The Faith Mission, 1960), p. 17.

Chapter 13

Titles of the Sermon

'A Spiritual Advancement'

'A Moral Improvement'

'An Annual Assessment of Spiritual Progress.'

'Duties of a Man of God'.

Scripture

I Timothy 6:3-16

Genesis 13:2, 8-11; 14:6; 26:12-14; 39:2-4

Deuteronomy 33:1

Ruth 2:11-12

I Samuel 12:22

II Samuel 9:3-7

I Kings 12:22

I Chronicles 28:11- 19: 29:10-13

II Chronicles 1:7-12, 22; 17:8

Job 1:1-3, 21; 2:10

Psalms 58:11; 91

Proverbs 11:3-6, 18

Matthew 6: 2-6, 13-14, 19-21, 31-33

Luke 16:9

John 15:18-19; 17:14-16

Romans 4:3, 22

I Corinthians 10:24; 15:12-18

Galatians 3:6

II Thessalonians 2:9-12

II Timothy 1:2; 3:17

Text: I Timothy 6:11

A Few Versions of the Text, I Timothy 6:11

But thou, man of God, flee these things; and follow after righteousness, godliness, faith, love, patience, meekness. *King James Version.*

But thou, O man of God, flee these things; and follow after righteousness, godliness, faith, love, patience, meekness. *Explanatory Notes Upon the New Testament*

But as for you, man of God, shun all this; aim at righteousness, godliness, faith, love, steadfastness, gentleness. *Revised Standard Version*

But you, man of God, flee from all this; and pursue righteousness, godliness, faith, love, endurance, gentleness. *New International Version*

But you, man of God, must shun all this; and pursue justice, piety, fidelity, love, fortitude, gentleness. *The New English Bible*

Oh, Timothy, you are God's man. Run from all these evil things and work instead as what is right and good, learning to trust him and love others, and to be patient and gentle. *The Living Bible Illustrated*

But you, man of God, must avoid these things. Pursue what God approves of a godly life, faith, love, endurance, and gentleness. *God's Word*

Introduction

I humbly consider my participation with you, when you are celebrating the one hundred sixty second (162nd) Church anniversary, as my honourable privilege. I give thanks to my Lord and Saviour, Jesus Christ for this unique opportunity of sharing some principles of the gospel with the congregation. I believe that God inspired your ministers

and their advisory board to invite me as a preacher. This is the first
invitation of your congregation, after I gave up the position of being
the general superintendent in 1998. Let today's message be acceptable
to the Lord and His faithful followers. Let me repeat the plea of King
David, saying:

> Let the word of my mouth and the mediation of my heart be acceptable in
> thy sight, O LORD, my rock and my redeemer. (Ps. 19:14)

Let this message be for glory and pleasure of the LORD God rather
than pleasing into sight of man. Let my meditation be in accordance
with the word of God rather than politically acceptable to man's
expectation and thoughts.

Introduction of the Text

Each anniversary of the congregation or church, regardless its size
and numbers, be an opportunity to assess how the church has advanced
materially and spiritually; and how each believer is personally advanced
materially and spiritually. How many souls are won for God in Jesus
Christ through the evangelical work of the church and its believers?
How all believers have influenced the society at large; and spread the
gospel among the nonbelievers? We personally wish and want to
advance materially and spiritually. We collectively think the same for
our church.

I believe that material advancement and spiritual progress should
go hand in hand. When believers practise justice and righteousness,
the LORD God blesses them in whatever they undertake. For example,
God was with Joseph, who had fear of God in his heart, and thereby
who overcame sexual temptation; therefore, the LORD God prospered
Joseph in whatever he was doing. (Gen. 39:2-4) He was elevated to
the position next to the king of Egypt from being a slave. All patriarchs,
who walked with the LORD God, were wealthy or rich persons. This
is a general impression of the word of God, the Bible, exclusively.
We will reflect on what the Bible teaches about the relationship
between righteousness and material prosperity in the process of
delivering the message.

Most of the Canadians believe that free enterprise system is good for them and for Canada. They have ventured and gained wealth. We congratulate them for being rich and prosperous. They have freedom to establish a chain of grocery stores, pharmacies, edibles, banks, and insurance companies, etc. They can be wealthy by expanding their business. But one should ask a few questions: Are those entrepreneurs spiritually progressed? Do they follow moral principles of doing fair and just business? Do you have pleasant experiences with the wealthy businessmen? Do they share their wealth with the poor and needy? There might be a few exceptions with reference of doing charitable works. We are informed that many firms became rich by dishonest and fraudulent ways and means. For example, oil companies and the government are making money by artificially creating shortage of oil. Banks are making profits in billions by charging various fees to the customers. Insurance companies make profits in billions. Their economic massive growth has been possible, because they do not wish and will to follow moral guidelines. The believers should know or they know that there are spiritual and ethical dangers when firms and persons advance materially by ignoring their own spiritual progress. Some evangelists, Jim Orsen Baker and Tammy Fae of the Praise the Lord club, were involved in defrauding some Christians in millions of dollars. Jim Orsen Baker (January 2, 1940-...) was sentenced imprisonment for forty-five years (45) in 1991; his sentence was reduced to eighteen years; and he was released in 1995. He served the time for his crimes of corruption. He wandered away from the faith and brought sufferings upon himself. We know the Enron foundation was made bankrupt by their executives and an executive committed suicide and others are serving time. There are many such events in the history of the U. S. A.

Let us search the Bible and find out what the word of God teaches about being affluent or rich and progressive in spiritual and moral life. Let us try to find a text from the Bible which would exhort us today as to what should be our ultimate preference. St. Paul in his exhortation to Timothy, his spiritual child (II Tim. 1:2), wrote Timothy about the alternative to love of money or pursuit of worldly riches, saying:

> **But as for you, man of God, shun all this; aim at righteousness, godliness, faith, love, steadfastness, gentleness.** (I Timothy 6:11)

This is the text of our meditation today.

The Context of the Text

St. Paul wrote these words of the text to Timothy, who was an evangelist and a pastor or a bishop of the church. There were some teachers in the churches, who were teaching new doctrines, which were against the doctrines preached by the apostles, including St. Paul. The apostolic doctrines were intended to produce practical holiness for believers and the society. On the contrary, the doctrines which were preached by the false teachers, were alienating believers from Jesus Christ, because those doctrines were not given by God in Jesus Christ, and they were originated with men. They were not promoting holiness and morality among the believers and in society. They were promoting their personal interests. Let us go back to the scripture lesson in order to know how a false teacher was described and what were undesirable effects of his teaching:

> He is puffed up with conceit, he knows nothing; he has a morbid craving for controversy and for disputes about words, which produce envy, dissension, slander, base suspicions, and wrangling among men who are depraved in mind and bereft of the truth, imagining that godliness is a means of gain. (I Tim. 6:4-5)

In short, the false teachers were interested in doctrinal disputes, divisions in the body of the church, and hatred among the believers, because those doctrines were not divine but were man-made. Those teachers were corrupt. St. Paul described their spiritual condition somewhere, as follows:

> The coming of the lawless one by the activity of Satan...and with all wicked deception for those who are to perish, because they refused to love the truth and be saved. Therefore, God sends upon them a strong delusion, to make them believe what is false, so that all may be condemned who do not believe the truth but had pleasure in unrighteousness. (II Thes. 2:9-12)

In other words, the doctrines of false teachers were satanic and against holiness. Therefore, they were imagining that godliness was a means of material gain.

Timothy was an apostolic preacher. He had to be truthful and faithful to the apostolic doctrines; and to uphold them, because they were intended to produce moral and spiritual holiness. Therefore, St. Paul exhorted and suggested the alternative to the lifestyle of the false teachers, saying to Timothy:

> But as for you, man of God, shun all this; aim at righteousness, godliness, faith, love, steadfastness, gentleness. (I Timothy 6:11)

This is the text, within its social, moral, and theological setting.

An Analysis of the Text

In this text, there are two sets of duties for the man of God. Therefore, the text has two ideas. (A) The first idea is a negative sets of duties. St. Paul exhorted Timothy to shun or avoid all this, because he was a man of God.

(B) The second idea of the text is a positive set of duties. St. Paul exhorted Timothy to aim at or pursue righteousness, godliness, faith, love, steadfastness, and gentleness.

An Exposition of the Ideas of the Text

(A) The first idea is that St. Paul exhorted Timothy to shun or avoid all this, because he was a man of God. St. Paul knew that Timothy was a man of God, or chosen servant of Jesus Christ. St. Paul addressed Timothy saying, "O man of God." This typical expression is found in the Old Testament. Moses was addressed so in Dt. 33:1; a messenger to Eli who was a main priest at Shiloh, before Samuel was addressed so in I Sam. 2:27 and Shemaiah, a messenger to King Rehoboam (922-915 B. C.) was addressed so in I Kings 12:22. St. Paul used the expression to Timothy intending Timothy to be as representing responsible church leaders. (Cf. II Tim. 3:17) Rev. John Wesley interpreted "a man of God" which means either a prophet, a messenger of God, or a man devoted to God: a man of another world.

God in Jesus Christ expects every minister of His church to be a man of God.

A first obligatory responsibility of the man of God in Jesus Christ is to avoid the lifestyle of ungodly or devilish men. This is a negative categorical imperative for godly men. What were the features of the ungodly lifestyle of the false teachers, which must be avoided? Let us reflect on a few of those features.

(1) First, the false teachers were teaching new or rather wrong doctrines in the church of Jesus Christ. Instead of teaching the apostolic doctrines, they were preaching their own doctrines. They were authors or originators of those doctrines. In formulating their doctrines, they rejected the sound words of the apostles, even the words of the Lord Jesus Christ. By rejection of the sound words of even of Jesus Christ, they were alienating the believers from the Lord and Saviour Jesus Christ. The result of teaching those unbiblical doctrines was moral chaos or disintegration among the believers.

(2) Secondly, the false teachers were not men of truth. They were not debating to reveal and establish truth of the gospel of Jesus Christ. They were interested in questioning the truth and quarrelling over the words. They wanted to leave impression on the audience how logical and intellectual they were. They did not care for distorting truth to serve their interests. Their minds were not pure but corrupt. They were puffed up, filled with pride and spiritual darkness. They did not know the truth. They were without truth.

(3) Thirdly, the false teachers were interested in wranglings or irritating quarrels. Their wranglings created divisions among the believers; and created social condition, conducing impiety and moral disintegration.

(4) Fourthly, the false teachers were speculating or imagining that godliness is a way of gain. They did not think of pursuit of material wealth would cause any danger to spirituality and social morality. They had developed strong love for material things, and especially

for money. St. Paul issued a solemn warning to the believers against the love of money and pursuit of material prosperity. Let us go back to our scripture lesson and read verses from 6 to 10.

> There is great gain in godliness with contentment; for we brought nothing into the world, and we cannot take anything out of the world; but if we have food and clothing, with these we shall be content. But those who desire to be rich fall into temptation, into a snare, into many senseless and hurtful desires that plunge men into ruin and destruction. For the love of money is the root of all evils; it is through this craving that some have wandered away from the faith and pierced their hearts with many pangs. (I Tim. 6:6-10)

This is the teaching of both Old and New Testament. There were many patriarchs, whom God provided all material things in abundance. Abraham was a patriarch. He was very rich in cattle, in silver, and in gold (Gen. 13:2). He was not greedy; therefore he allowed his nephew Lot to choose the land for his settlement and to avoid possible strifes between him and Lot and between their herdsmen. Lot chose Jorden valley, which was well watered and fertile (Gen. 13:8-11). Abraham and Lot separated one from the other, in peace.

Isaac, a son of Abraham was another patriarch. He inherited all wealth from his father. Isaac obeyed God and God caused him to prosper so much so that the Philistines became envious of Isaac (Gen. 26:12-14).

There are some kings whom God caused to prosper; for example, David, and his son Solomon. God was with David, because David obeyed God. God made David the king of all tribes of Israel (1002-962 B. C.). God made him a rich king. However, King David did not become greedy. He found out Mephibosheth, a son of Jonathan, who was a son of King Saul (1044-1004 B. C.). He restored the land of Saul to him; and made him to dine at his royal table (II Sam. 9:3-7). David planned to build the first temple for the LORD God; and gave abundant things for building the temple (I Chr. 28:11-19). King David blessed the LORD God for his riches and honour (I Chr. 29:10-13).

Solomon was a son of King David; he inherited his father's wealth. God was pleased with Solomon, when King Solomon (962-922 B. C.) asked the LORD God to give him wisdom and understanding to govern the people. God granted his request and added all riches to him; God promised Solomon to make him a greatest king among other kings. (II Chr. 1:7-12)

The LORD God made His faithful servants rich. Job was upright; he had fear of God in his heart; therefore, he turned away from evil; and did charitable deeds always. God was pleased with Job. He made Job, a richest man among the people of the east (Job 1:1-3). Satan knew that God had protected all that Job had. Satan asked God to remove the divine protection; then Job would curse God. God permitted Satan to test the faith of Job. Satan brought all kinds of calamities and destroyed all possessions, his children, and servants. When everything was taken away from Job, Job humbled himself and praised God, saying:

> Naked I came from mother's womb, and naked shall I return; the LORD gave, and the LORD has taken away; blessed be the name of the LORD. (Job. 1:21)

Job did not curse God, when he became extremely poor and without any means for survival. Then Satan brought a sickness on Job to test his faith further. When Job was in a miserable condition, his wife advised him to curse God and die. He responded to her, saying:

> You speak as one of the foolish women would speak. Shall we receive good at the hand of God, and shall we not receive evil? (Job 2:10)

What can we learn from these examples of the Old Testament? First, God provides His faithful servants, when they trust Him and His providence, and when they obey Him and His commandments. Jesus Christ endorsed this thought, when He exhorted His audience, saying:

> Therefore do not be anxious, saying, 'What shall I eat?' or 'what shall I drink?' or 'What shall we wear?' For the Gentiles seek all these things; and your heavenly Father knows you need them all. But seek first his kingdom and his righteousness, and all these things shall be yours as well. (Mt. 6:31-33)

As far accumulation of riches, Jesus Christ said early to the people:

> Do not lay up for yourselves treasures on earth, where moth and rust consume
> and where thieves break in and steal, but lay up for yourselves treasures in
> heaven, where neither moth nor rust consumes and where thieves do not
> break in and steal. For where your treasure is, there will your heart be also.
> (Mt. 6:19-21)

Secondly, material riches are to be used for gaining spiritual wealth.
When God makes man rich or prosperous, He makes man not an owner
but a steward of wealth. A rich man or woman has to use wealth for
the well-being of the poor, destitute, orphans, widows. Material riches
were called unrighteous mammon by Jesus Christ. Jesus Christ exhorted
the people, saying:

> And I tell you, make friends for yourselves by means of unrighteous
> mammon, so that when it fails they may receive you into the eternal
> habitations. (Lk. 16:9)

Thirdly, the persons who desire to be rich or who are greedy for worldly
things, use unethical means and ways to amass wealth. They are not
mindful of hurting others for their gain. They cannot become happy
and content. They become evil. The composer of the book of
Proverbs wrote as follows:

> The integrity of the upright guides them, but the crookedness of the
> treacherous destroys them. Riches do not profit in the day of wrath, but
> righteousness delivers from death. The righteousness of the blameless keeps
> his way straight, but the wicked falls by his own wickedness. The righteousness
> of the upright delivers them, but the treacherous are taken captive by their
> lust. (Pr. 11:3-6)

Rev. John Wesley (1703-1791) delivered a sermon # 87 on "The
Danger of Riches," based on I Timothy 6:9:

> But those who desire to be rich fall into temptation, into a snare; into many
> senseless and hurtful desires that plunge men into ruin and destruction.

In that sermon, Rev. Wesley interpreted that whatever is more than
food and coverings is riches; or whatever is above the plain necessities
of life is riches. Whoever has sufficient food to eat, and clothes to
put on, and a place where to lay his head, and something over, is rich.
Anyone, who desires more than what is sufficient, is desiring to be

rich. Everyone is guilty of this kind of sin   Very few escape from the temptation of being rich. They fall into the snare of the devil. They fall into many foolish and hurtful desire, hurtful both to the mind and spirit. They become lovers of pleasures more than lovers of God. They become drunkard and glutton. They desire honour, the esteem, admiration, and applause of men. They desire to avoid every cross, every degree of trouble, danger, and difficulty. They finally are drawn in pain and disease. Rev. Wesley exhorted the people to give to God's work whatever is more than sufficient, as a faithful and wise stewards. The rich people give up their faith. They hurt their neighbours. They have no contentment. Having summarised the sermon of Rev. John Wesley in short, let me go back to the scripture lesson and refer to the exhortation of St. Paul to all Christians, saying:

> There is a great gain in godliness with contentment; for we brought nothing into the world, and we cannot take anything out of the world; but if we have food and clothing, with these we shall be content. (I Tim. 6:6-8)

In short, a man of God should not be a lover of money and other material things, power and prestige. This is a negative duty of a man of God.

When the first holy club at Orford was formed, it was the practice of those Methodists to give away each year all they had after providing for their own necessities. Rev. John Wesley, having thirty pounds a year, lived on twenty-eight, and gave away two. The next year, receiving sixty pounds, he still lived on twenty-eight; and gave away thirty-two. The third year he received ninety pounds; and gave away sixty-two. The fourth year he received one hundred and twenty pounds; and still lived on twenty-eight as before, giving the the poor all the rest.   Rev. John Wesley was a man of God, who was content with supply of his basic necessities; and who practised the principle of charity throughout his life. He did not desire to be rich in worldly things. He was unselfish and charitable to others. He followed the scripture which says: "Let no one seek his own good, but the good of his neighbour." (I Cor. 10:24) He cared for the wellbeing of his colleagues and the poor. Therefore, God blessed his ministry tremendously. Rev. John Wesley was a living example for the people called Methodists. He can be our example also.

(B) The second idea is that St. Paul exhorted to Timothy to aim at or pursue righteousness, godliness, faith, love, steadfastness, and gentleness. This is a positive set of duties of a man of God. There are three pairs of virtues, which the man of God has to pursue.

(1) The first pair is of righteousness and goodness. This pair is opposite of unrighteousness and wickedness, which are the sources of sins. The LORD God is holy, just and good. He expects of man to be in His image or to walk in His disciplined way. He rewards the righteous and punishes the wicked. The word of God is filled with this teaching:

When Ruth went to glean in the field of Boaz, he said to her:

All that you have done for your mother-in-law since the death of your husband has been fully told me, and how you left your father and mother and your native land and came to a people that you did not know before. The LORD recompense you for what you have done, and a full reward be given by the LORD, the God of Israel, under whose wings you have come to take refuge. (Ruth 2:11-12)

King David wrote in a psalm:

Men will say, 'Surely there is a reward for the righteous; surely there is a God who judges on earth.' (Ps. 58:11)

King Solomon,the complier of the Proverbs wrote:

A wicked man earns deceptive wages, but one who sows righteousness gets a sure reward. He who is steadfast in righteousness will live, but he who pursues evil will die. (Pr. 11:18-19)

Jesus Christ, in His Sermon on the Mountain, exhorted the people to fast in secret and to give alms in secret, because God will reward them for those deeds. (Mt. 6:2-3).

Believers in Jesus Christ have to choose the practice of righteous way; and their rewards would follow them. God will protect them from all kinds of evil; and provide them everything in abundance. This religious conviction is confirmed in Ps. 91:1-16. When the people will seek righteousness and godliness, all things will be given to them as rewards, without their asking or pursuing. It was true in case of Rev. John Wesley.

(2) The second pair is of faith and love. This pair is opposite of disbelief or doubts and hatred. They are the sources of distrust and hatred toward God and man. Hatred and distrust are evils or sins.

The pair of faith and love are the fundamental to Christian belief. This pair is associated with the first pair of righteousness and goodness. Righteousness is the offspring of faith; and godliness is the offspring of love. We can see this assumption true in case of Abraham. Abraham had faith in the LORD God; he believed in the promises of God. I assume you know those divine promises to Abraham. Therefore, Abraham's trust or faith was counted as righteousness. It is written in the scripture: "Abraham believed the LORD and He reckoned it to him as righteousness." (Gen. 14:6) St. Paul quoted this verse in his letter to the Romans (4:3, 22) and to the Letter to Galatians (Gal. 3:6) to argue the point that righteousness is based on trust in God. Abraham was good even to the strangers, because he was practising right relationship with God and man. He entertained three strangers as his guests (Gen. 18:1-8). He was truly a good man, because he loved the LORD God.

(3) The third pair is of steadfastness and gentleness. This pair is opposite of impatience and arrogance. Impatience and arrogance are vices or evil tempers. Believers in Christ are not of the world; therefore, the world would hate them and persecute them, as it had done with Jesus Christ (Jn 17:14-16; 15:18-19; 8:23). The believers have to lead their spiritual and moral life in the world which provokes them. Christians are persecuted and murdered in the countries where Hindus, Budhist, and Muslim are predominant people. Christians in other countiries will have to resist the opposition from the world by being firm in their faith and being gentle. Recently somebody who is a journalist and not an archaeologist claimed that he discovered the tomb of and bones of Jesus Christ. This is an arrogant and preposterous, utterly absurd claim. This is a deliberate and senseless attack on the belief of the Christians in the resurrection of Jesus Christ

and their belief in the resurrection of all. We know that the tomb was empty when Jesus Christ was resurrected. Our faith had been supported by historical facts concerning the resurrection of Jesus Christ. Let no one create a doubt or a suspicion in the minds of true Christians. Let me quote from the scripture which says: "If Christ has not been raised, your faith is futile and you are still in your sins." (I Cor. 15:17)   In simple words, it means that our salvation from sin is dependent on the resurrection of Jesus Christ. There is no victory over sin and death, if Jesus Christ was not resurrected. The belief in the resurrection of Jesus Christ is very vital to Christians. The preaching becomes in vain and so our faith and testimony of God. (I Cor. 15:14-15) They must defend themselves from this kind of doctrianal attack from a scholar or a fool.

Conclusion

Let us go back to the text and apply the principles coming out of the text. It teaches not to love money or pursue worldly riches, because there are spiritual and moral dangers in the pursuit. On the contrary, it teaches to pursue righteousness and godliness, because other material things will be given to us by God. Therefore, let us reflect on the questions such as: Am I a lover of money or of worldly things? Am I content when my basic needs-suficeint food, clothes, and shelter-are met? Do I know the dangers of going after worldly things- money, prestige, power? Do I look after my interest only or do I think of the interests of others? Do I want all gravy on my plate? Do I care that other fellows have something or nothing on their plates? Do I follow moral or just ways when I get worldly things from others? Do I think that God will hold me accountable for my deeds? Do I believe in the final divine judgment when I will be rewarded for my good deeds? and do I believe that I will be punished for my evil deeds? Am I doing charitable deeds for the poor and needy, because God has made me a steward of my possession?

Let us reflect on the questions such as: Is my church a selfish institute? Is my church doing charitable deeds? Is my church winning souls for Christ? Does my church play dirty politics in grabbing powerful positions in the church and in the Conference?

A congregation of Jesus Christ must pursue righteousness and godliness in order to be blessed by God. Each congregation must have moral standard when it participates in administration. Jesus Christ compared His followers with light and salt of the earth (Mt.6:13-14), giving them a mission of maintainng a moral standard in the world. Every true believer must see that his or her congregation is first of all growing spiritually and keeping moral principles, based on the word of God. This is a bounden duty of every minister and every true Christian. May God in Jesus Christ bless everyone with this understanding, when he or she participate in the anniversary of the church. God bless you all according to His will and pleasure.

Recommended Hymns from the Methodist Hymnal

34   'Immortal, invisible, God only wise'

64   'Praise to the Lord, the Almighty,'

70   'All my hope on God is founded'

490   'Fight the good fight with all thy might;'

492   'I the good fight have fought,'

498   'Rock of Ages, cleft for me,'

Recommended Responsive Reading from A Worship Manual for Scriptural or Methodist Order of Service

63 (pp.167-168),

88 (pp.210-211),

89 (pp. 211-213),

125 (pp.285-286).

Bibliography

A) Primary Sources

The Holy Bible, King James Version. Goedonville, Tennessee: Dugan Publishers, Inc., 1984

The Holy Bible, Revised Standard Version. London,Edinburgh,Paris,Melbourne, Johannesburg,Toronto,and New York: Thomas Nelson and Sons Ltd.,12th impression, 1962.

The Thompson Chain-Reference Bible, New International Version. Grand Rapids, Michigan: Zondervan Bible Publishers, second printing, 1983.

The New English Bible with the Apocrypha. New York: Oxford University Press, 1971.

The Way, The Living Bible Illustrated. Wheaton, Illinois: Tyndale House Publishers, sixth printing, 1973.

God's Word, Today's Bible translation that says what it means. Grand Rapids, Michigan: World Publishing Ins., 1995.

B) Secondary Sources

Barckay, William. *The Mind of St Paul*. London & Glasgow: Collins Fontana books, 1965.

—————————. *The Letter to the Hebrews*. Edinburgh: The Saint Andrew Press, 5th Impression, 1963.

—————————. *The Letters to the Corinthians*. Edinburgh: The Saint Andre Press, fifth impression, 1961.

—————————. *The Gospel of Luke*. Edinburgh: The Saint Andrew Press, Eighth Impression, 1964.

Grayzel, Solomon. *A History of the Jews*. New York and Scarborough, Ontario: The Jewish Publication Society of America, New Revised Ed., 1968.

Johnson, Paul. *A History of the Modern World from 1917 to the 1990s*. London: Weidenfeld and Nicolson, revised edition, 1983.

Josephus. *The Works of Josephus*, complete and unabridged. tr. W. Whiston. U. S. A. : Hendrickson Publisher, ninth printing, 1994.

Kruse, Colin G. *The Second Epistle of Paul to the Corinthians*. Grand Rapids, Michigan: William B. Eerdmans Publishing Company, reprinted, 1991.

The Methodist Hymn Book with Office. London : The Methodist Publishing House, 1933.

Methodist Preacher, *John Wesley the Methodist: A Plain Account of His life and Work*. New York: Eaton & Mains, 1903.

Miller, Basil. *William Carey: The Father o Modern Missions*. Minneapolis, Minnesota: Bethany House Publishers, 1980.

Osbeck, Kenneth W. *101 Hymn Stories*. Grand Rapids,Michigan:Kregal Publications, 1982.

Power, M., and Butler, N. *Slavery and Freedom in Niagara*. Niagra-on-the Lake, Ontario: The Niagra Historical Society, 1993.

Plummer, Alfred. *A Critical and Exegetical Commentary on the Gospel According to St. Luke.* "*The International Critical Commentary.*" New York: Charles Scribner's Sons, 1896.

Spear, Percival. *A History of India*. Harmondsworth,Middlesex, England: Penguin Books, Reprinted 1973. Vol. II

Sproul, R. C. *The Holiness of God*. Wheaton,Illinois:Tyndale House Publishers, Inc., 1985.

Trumbull, H. Clay. *The Blood Covenant*. Kirkwood: Impact Books Inc., 1975.

Wesley, John. *The Works of John Wesley*. Grand Rapids, Michigan: Baker Book House, 3rd Ed. 1984. Vol.14

——————.*Explanatory Notes Upon the New Testament*. Grand Rapids, Michigan: Baker Book House, 1986. Vol.2

The Wesleyan Bible Commentary. Peabody, Massachusetts: Hendrickson Publishers. reprinted 1986. Vol.6

C) Other Sources

Mead, Frank S. ed. *The Encyclopedia of Religious Quotations*. Old Tappan, New Jersey: Fleming H. Revell Company, 1965.

Neill, S., Goodwin, J., and Dowle, A., ed. *Concise Dictionary of the Bible*. London: United Society for Christian Literature, Lutterworth Press, 1966. Vol. 2.

The New American Encyclopedia. Philadelphia: The Publisher Agency Inc., 1974. Vol. 20.

Tan, Paul Lee. *Encyclopedia of 7700 Illustrations: Signs of the Times*. Rockville,Maryland: Assurance Publishers, 9th printing, 1985.

Appendix - 1

Rt. Rev. Dr. Daniel D. Rupwate has written more than three hundred textual sermons. Some of his textual sermons are published in the books, having different titles, mentioned below. This index booklet includes only fifteen books. Other sermons were privately published; they are excluded from the list. The index will help readers know where his textual sermons be found.

Index Booklet for the Published Sermons

Name of the Book	Book Number
In Remembrance of the Life- Blood of Jesus Christ: Thirty-Six Textual Sermons on the Holy Communion	1
A Meditation on Good Friday: Textual Sermons on Seven Utterances of Jesus Christ from the Cross	2
The Good News of the Bible: Twenty-Five Textual Sermons on the Gospel Of and About Jesus Christ Vol. I	3
The Good News of the Bible: Twenty-Five Textual Sermons on the Gospel Of and About Jesus Christ Vol. II	4
Proven Divinity of Jesus Christ Through His Spiritual Titles and Exclusive claims	
A Biblical Perspective on Mothers' Day, Fathers' Day and Children's Day	6
Biblical Foundations of Scripturally Based Spiritual Revival in the Church: Twenty-Eight Textual Sermons on Revivals and Reforms	7

Text	Book No.	Chapter No.
Genesis		
2:18	12	8
4:9	9	20
22:16-18	14	1
24:50-51	12	9
Exodus		
4:13	9	1
14:15-16	9	2
20:12	6	7
Leviticus		
23:23-24	14	2
13:30	7	1
13:30	15	12
Deuteronomy		
5:15	7	2
8:10	15	1
8:14	7	3
16:14	14	3
32:6	15	2
Joshua		
23:14	12	15
I Samuel		
2:20	6	1
12:24-25	10	2
I Kings		
19:12	4	2
19:12	10	3
II Kings		
4:10	6	2

Text	Book No.	Chapter No.
II Kings		
12:15	9	20
17:15	7	4
20:5-6	7	5
23:3	7	6
23:3	14	4
23:3	10	4
I Chronicles		
29:17	15	3
II Chronicles		
32:7-8	7	7
34:31	14	5
Nehemiah		
9:28	11	1
Psalms		
24:3-4	11	2
26:1	10	5
50:23	15	4
51:10	11	3
73:25	12	16
82:3-4	9	21
103:2-5	15	5
Psalms		
111:10	10	6
112:5-6	12	17
116:15	12	18
119:9	6	13
121:1-2	11	4
127:1	12	10

Text	Book No.	Chapter No.
Proverbs		
2:12	6	14
3:27	9	22
9:10	7	8
10:1	6	15
10:7	12	19
11:24	15	6
13:21	9	23
19:18	6	16
20:7	6	8
22:6	6	17
23:13-14	6	9
24:3	7	9
25:4-5	9	24
29:15	6	3
29:15	6	18
29:18	9	25
31:20	6	4
31:30	6	5
Ecclesiastes		
12:13-14	10	7
Isaiah		
4:4	11	5
11:1	7	10
11:1	9	3
25:8	12	20
28:26	9	26
32:17	9	27
66:3	12	21

Text	Book No.	Chapter No.
Jeremiah		
5:30-31	10	8
18:4	11	6
Ezekiel		
11:19-20	14	6
34:4	9	28
Hosea		
6:1-2	12	22
Amos		
3:7	9	4
5:24	9	29
Micah		
5:2	13	1
Habakkuk		
3:17-18	15	7
Haggai		
1:9-10	9	5
2:9	15	8
Zechariah		
4:6	7	1
Matthew		
1:1	5	1
1:21	13	2
1:23	13	3
2:3	13	4
2:10-11	13	5
2:12	13	6
3:11	12	1
5:13	8	2

Text	Book No.	Chapter No.
Matthew		
5:14-15	8	3
5:17	4	3
5:20	9	6
7:14	8	3
7:18-19	8	5
7:25	8	6
7:28-29	3	2
8:8	7	12
8:17	3	3
9:17	8	7
10:32-33	4	4
12:45	8	8
13:8	8	9
13:9	3	4
13:30	8	10
13:32	8	11
13:44	8	12
13:45-46	8	13
13:47	8	14
13:52	8	15
16:16	5	2
16:23	4	5
18:35	8	16
19:14	12	2
20:16	8	17
20:31	8	18
21:8	13	17
21:9	13	18

Text	Book No.	Chapter No.
Matthew		
21:13	10	9
21:16	13	19
21:41	8	19
21:42	3	5
22:12	8	20
25:13	8	21
25:40	9	30
25:45	9	31
25:45-46	8	22
26:27	1	1
26:29	1	2
26:38	11	7
26:64	5	3
26:66	11	8
27:46	2	4
Mark		
1:14-15	4	6
1:22	3	6
4:26-29	8	23
8:35	4	7
10:30	4	8
11:9-10	13	20
16:3	13	24
Luke		
2:7	13	7
2:10	13	8
2:11	13	9
2:21	13	10
2:34-35	13	11

Text	Book No.	Chapter No.
Luke		
2:52	6	19
2:21	12	3
4:18-19	3	7
5:4-5	7	13
7:32	8	24
7:47	8	25
9:62	4	9
10:36-37	8	26
11:9	8	27
12:21	8	28
12:48	8	29
13:5	11	9
13:8-9	8	30
13:21	8	31
13:24	8	32
14:11	8	33
14:28	8	34
15:7	8	35
15:10	8	36
15:32	8	37
16:10	8	38
16:15	10	10
16:25	8	39
17:18	15	9
18:7-8	8	40
18:14	8	41
19:26	8	42
21:3	15	10
22:13	1	3

Text	Book No.	Chapter No.
Luke		
22:15	1	4
22:20	1	5
23:24	2	1
23:42-43	2	2
23:46	2	7
24:5	13	25
24:30-31	1	6
24:46-47	3	8
John		
1:14	5	4
1:14	13	12
2:17	13	21
3:3	7	14
3:16	3	9
3:30	13	13
4:13-14	5	7
4:21	11	10
4:26	5	5
4:42	9	7
6:35	5	8
6:35	1	7
6:53	1	8
8:12	5	9
8:31-32	7	15
8:42	6	10
8:58	5	10
10:7	5	11
10:11	10	11
10:11	5	12

Text	Book No.	Chapter No.
John		
11:25	5	13
12:5	9	32
12:9	13	22
12:14-15	13	23
12:35-36	12	23
13:13	5	6
13:15	9	8
13:18	1	9
14:6	5	14
15:4	7	16
15:10	6	11
15:13-14	1	10
19:26-27	2	3
19:28	2	5
19:30	2	6
21:12	1	11
21:15	13	26
21:18-19	13	27
Acts		
6:3	9	9
19:5-6	12	4
20:24	4	10
20:28	1	12
Romans		
1:16-17	3	10
2:29	14	7
3:25	1	13
5:8	3	11
5:9	1	14

Text	Book No.	Chapter No.
Romans		
5:18	3	12
6:4	12	5
8:18	12	24
10:15	4	11
12:2	7	17
12:9	10	12
13:12-13	4	12
15:18	10	13
16:18	10	14
I Corinthians		
10:16	1	17
10:21	1	18
10:33-11:1	7	19
11:26	1	19
11:29	1	20
13:5	12	11
15:17	13	28
II Corinthians		
2:15-16	3	15
3:9	3	16
4:3-4	3	17
4:6	3	18
4:18	12	25
5:15	1	21
5:17	14	8
5:20-21	3	19
7:10	11	12
9:8	15	11

Text	Book No.	Chapter No.
Galatians		
1:9	4	16
1:11-12	3	20
2:20	4	17
2:20	7	20
3:13	3	21
4:4-5	4	18
5:1	4	19
Ephesians		
1:13-14	4	20
2:13	1	22
2:15-16	3	22
3:6	3	23
3:17-18	13	14
4:3	9	33
4:5	12	6
4:11-12	9	13
5:2	14	9
5:8-9	13	15
Philippians		
1:27-28a	3	24
2:4	9	14
2:9	9	15
3:10-11	13	29
3:13-14	11	13
3:13-14	9	16
Colossians		
1:13-14	1	23
1:23	4	21
1:20	1	24

Text	Book No.	Chapter No.
Colossians		
1:28	4	22
2:12	13	30
3:14	12	12
I Thessalonians		
2:3-4	3	25
5:5:11	9	17
II Thessalonians		
2:15	4	23
I Timothy		
6:11	15	13
II Timothy		
1:5	6	6
1:10	4	24
2:21	11	14
3:5	7	21
3:15	6	20
4:21	9	18
Titus		
2:11-12	7	22
2:11-12	11	15
Hebrews		
2:11	13	16
2:14	1	25
4:9-10	12	26
8:6	1	26
9:14	1	27
9:22	1	28
10:19-20	1	29
11:9-1	12	27

Text	Book No.	Chapter No.
Hebrews		
12:5-6	6	12
13:4	12	13
13:12	1	30
James		
2:13	7	24
3:17	7	25
I Peter		
1:2	1	31
1:12	4	25
1:17	10	17
1:18-19	1	32
2:24-25	3	26
3:21	12	7
4:17	4	26
II Peter		
1:5-7	4	27
1:8	4	28
I John		
1:7	1	33
2:29	7	26
3:14	7	27
5:5	13	31
III John		
4	12	14
11	7	28
11	10	18
Revelation		
1:5-6	1	34
1:8	5	15

Text	Book No.	Chapter No.
Revelation		
3:16	9	19
5:9	1	35
7:1	1	36
7:16-17	12	28
21:7	12	29

Appendix - 2

The Prophets and the Kings
in the Old Testament

Before the kingdom of Israel was established, the LORD God chose priest Samuel to look after the spiritual welfare of the people of Israel. God asked Samuel to anoint Saul as the first king of the Israel. (I Sam. 10:1) The priest Samuel was also anointed as a prophet of the people of Israel. It means that prophethood originated with Samuel. King Saul failed to carry out a command of the LORD God, therefore God asked prophet Samuel to anoint David as the successor of King Saul (I Sam. 16:13). After King David, his son Solomon became the king of the Israel. After Solomon, his son Rehoboam became the king. During his period, the kingdom of Israel was divided. The southern kingdom was called the kingdom of Judah and the norther kingdom was called the kingdom of Israel. There kingdoms were destroyed by the foreign powers and Jews were taken into captivity. They settled in many parts of the world.

The Interpreters' Bible (volume I, pp. 145-148) has given a chart, detailing the names of the kingdoms of Judah and Israel and their dates of reigning. The chart also mentions the events after the destruction of those kingdoms. The chart, however, did not mention the names of the prophets against the names of the kings. It would useful to include the names of the prophets which would suggest their possible dates, along with the kings and the historical events.

The writer of the article is attempting to present a wider chart in order to include the prophets.

Prophet	King	
Samuel	Saul (1044-1004 B. C.)	
	David (1002-962 B. C.)	
Nathan (II Sam. 7:2)		
Gad (II Sam. 24:11)		
Nathan (I Kg. 1:32-34)	Solomon (962-922 B. C.)	
	King of Judah	King of Israel
	Rehoboam (922-915 B. C.)	Jeroboam (922-901)
	Abijam (915-913 B. C.)	Nadab (901-900 B. C.)
	Asa (913-873 B. C.)	Baasha (900-877 B. C.)
		Elah (877-876 B. C.)
		Zimri (876) 7 days
	Jehoshaphat (837-849 B. C.)	Omri (876-869 B. C.)
Elijah (I Kg. 18:2)		Ahab (869-850 B. C.)
Elisha (I Kg. 19:16)		
	King of Judah	King of Israel
		Ahaziah (850-849 B. C.)
	Jehoram (849-842 B. C.)	Joram (849-842 B. C.)
	Ahaziah (842 B. C.)	
	Athaliah (842-837 B. C.)	Jehu (842-815)
	(Queen)	
	Jehoash (837-800 B. C.)	Joahaz (815-801 B. C.)
	Amaziah (800-783 B. C.)	Joash (801-786 B. C.)
Isaiah (1:1)	Uzziah (Azariah) 783-742 B. C.)	Jeroboam (786-746 B. C.)
Amos (1:1)		
Micah (1:1)	Jotham (750-742 B. C.) regent	
Hosea (1:1)	Ahaz (735-715 (B. C.)	Jeroboam (786-746 B. C.)
		Zechariah (746-745 B. C.) 6 months
		Shallum (745 B. C.) 1 month
	Jotham (742-735 B. C.), king	Menahem (745-738 B. C.)
	Ahaz (735-715 B. C.)	Pekahia (738-737 B. C.)
		Pekah (737-732 B. C.)
		Hoshea (732-724 B. C.)
		Tiglath-pileser III of Assyria enthroned Hoshea in 732 B. C.
	King of Judah	
	Hezekiah (715-687 B. C.)	
Habakkuk	Manasseh (687-642 B. C.)	
	Amon (642-640 B. C.)	
Jeremiah (1:2)	Josiah (640-609 B. C.)	
Zephaniah (1:1)	Jehoahaz 609 B. C.) 3 months	
Daniel (1:1)	Jehoiakim (609-598 B. C.)	King Nebuchadnezer of Babylon (605-562 B. C.) besieged Jerusalem and King Jehoiakim was taken into captivity
Ezekiel (1:2)	Jehoiachin (598 B. C.) 3 months	
	Zedekiah (598-587 B. C.)	Jerusalem destroyed, Deportation of Jews
	Persian King	
	Cyrus (539-530 B. C.)	Edit for return of the Jews
Haggai (1:1)		Zerubbabel, governor of Judah (538-446 B.C.)
	Darius I (522-486 B. C.)	Work on the temple (520-516 B. C.)
	Artaxerxes I (465-424 B. C.)	Return of Ezra (548 B. C.)
	Nehemiah, governor of Judah (445-433 B. C.)	
Zechariah (1:1, 7; 7:1)	King Darius I (522-486 B. C.)	
	Artaxeres II (404-358 B. C.)	Return of Ezra (397 B. C.)

About the Author and the Book

The Rt. Rev. Dr. Daniel D. Rupwate, B. A. (Hons.), B. D., M. Th., Ph. D., was the General Superintendent of the British Methodist Episcopal Church of Canada from 1987 to 1998. He was born in Maharashtra (Bombay) State in India. He was graduated from the University Pune (Poona) in 1963 with B. A. (Hons.). As far as his training in a theology is concerned, he obtained B. D. in 1967 and M. Th. in 1970, from Senate of Serampore. Whilst in India, he served the Methodist Church in Southern Asia as a Minister in Nagpur, Poona, and Bombay. He was a lecturer in the United Theological College, Poona, for a year. He served as a Regional Secretary of Maharashtra State of the Christian Institute for the Study of Religion & Society. Some of his essays were published in a newspaper and were later compiled in a booklet in Marathi and published in 1974. The English subtitle for this booklet is A *Christianity in the Context of the Indian Way of Life*. In 1980 he obtained Ph. D. from McMaster University, Hamilton, Canada. He joined the ministry of the British Methodist Episcopal Church of Canada in 1978 and served as a Minister in Toronto, East York, Brantford, St. Catharines, and Niagara Falls, Ontario. He also served as the General Secretary of the B. M. E. Church Conference from 1982 to 1986. He wrote a few essays for Canadian Methodist Historical Society, which were published by the said organization. He continues to do research and writing on Methodism. His book A *Negro Methodist Churches, Rev. John Wesley's Thoughts Upon Slavery, and His Struggle Against Slavery* would help readers to know the significant contributions of the Rev. John Wesley, a founder of Methodism, toward propagating the gospel and combatting racism in the world.

While he was the General Superintendent, he took an initiative to revise and update ritual services and he completed the work and published *The Book of Offices for the British Methodist Episcopal Church* in 1998.

While holding the office of the General Superintendent, he also began to work on a worship manual for the B. M. E. Church. He has completed this work, it was published in 2005. I certainly hope that this book will enhance spirituality of devotional services.

He had been preaching textual sermons on every occasion. Some of those sermons were published under different titles of the books. (See the list of his published books) This book on thanksgiving is one of them. This book emphasizes biblical values behind celebrating Anniversary Services and Thanksgiving Services. I certainly hope that this book will confirm and strengthen the biblical values.

Rev. Dr. Kenneth Smith,

B. Sc., B. Ed., M. C. P., B. D., Ph. D.

Associate Professor, (Niagara University).

Other Works by the Author

Books

Jesus of Nazareth, the Messiah or Christ: Thirty-two Textual Sermons on Proving Jesus of Nazareth as Messiah or Christ, with an Essay, 'A Theological Significance of Forty Days' Delhi, India: ISPCK, 2018.

Sanctified, Sacred, and Saved Life of Christians: Twenty Nine Textual Sermons on Baptism, Matrimony, and Funeral, Delhi, India: ISPCK. 2018.

A Biblical Leadership and Church Discipline: Sixteen Textual Sermons, Delhi, India: ISPCK, 2017.

A Biblical Administration of the Church and Society: Nineteen Textual Sermons on Administration of the Church and Fifteen Textual Sermons on Administration of Society, Delhi, India: ISPCK, 2016.

The Teaching of Jesus Christ Through His Parables: Forty-one Textual Sermons on the Parables of Jesus Christ, Delhi, India: *ISPCK, 2016.*

Biblical Foundations of Scripturally Based Spiritual Revivals in the Church: Twenty Eight Textual Sermons on revivals and Reform and Rev. John Wesley's Theology of 'the New Birth', ISPCK, 2015.

A Biblical Perspective on Mothers' Day, Fathers' Day, and Children's Day, Delhi, India, ISPCK, 2014.

The Good News of the Bible: Twenty Five Textual Sermons on the Gospel of and About Jesus Christ, Vol. I, Delhi, India, ISPCK, 2014.

The Good News of the Bible: Twenty Seven Textual Sermons on the Gospel of and About Jesus Christ, Vol. I I, Delhi, India, ISPCK, 2014.

Proven Divinity of Jesus Christ Through His Scriptural Titles and Exceptional Claims, Delhi, India, ISPCK. 2014.

In Remembrance of the Life-Blood of Jesus Christ: Thirty-Six Textual Sermons on the Holy Communion, Pune India, The Word of Life Publication, 2003.

Negro Methodist Churches, Rev. John Wesley's Thoughts Upon Slavery, and His Struggle Against Slavery, 1998.

The Book of Offices for the British Methodist Episcopal Church, 1998.

A Worship Manual for a Scriptural or Methodist Order of Service, 2005.

Biblical Solutions to the Problems of a Church: Fifteen Textual Sermons, delivered at Annual and General Conferences of the B. M. E. Church of Canada, 1998.

A Scriptural Vindication of the Articles of Religion: Twenty-five Articles of Religion of Methodism with The Reverend John Wesley's Acts of and Thoughts about Baptism, 2010.

Booklets

A Meditation on Good Friday: Textual Sermons on Seven Utterances of Jesus Christ from the Cross, Pune, India: Sumitra Prakashan, 2012.

A Historical Significance of the "salem Chapel" with reference to the Underground Railroad Movement and a tribute to Harriet Tubman, Second or Revised edition, 2016.

Christianity in the Context of the Indian Way of Life (a book on social, religious, and political issues, in Marathi), Bangalore, India: Christian Institute for the Study of Region & Society, 1979.

Socio-Religious Policies of the British Methodist Episcopal Church of Canada, Toronto: B. M. E. Church Conference, 1990.

A Historical Significance of "Salem Chapel" with Reference to Underground Railroad Movement, 2006.

Essays

'The Bible and Racism', "Mukti", Bimonthly, Vol. 1, no. 4 and 5, Toronto, 1982, 1983.

Christian Participation in Politics', "Apostle", The B. M. E. Church of Canada Publication, May 1979.

The Covenant Theology of John Wesley, Toronto: Canadian Methodist Historical Society, 1993.

Methodist Piety and Social Morality or Scriptural Holiness of Methodism (Toronto: Canadian Methodist Historical Society, 1995).

A Versatile Significance of *Rta,* (Poona, India: Bhandarkar Oriental Research Institute, 1982).

Jesus of Nazareth, the Messiah, ISPCK, 1918, pp. 345-351.

'A Theological Significance of Forty Days,' Jesus of Nazareth, The Messiah or Christ: Thirty-two Textual Sermons on Proving Jesus of Nazareth as Messiah or Christ, with an Essay, 'Theological Significance of Forty Days,' ISPCK, 2018, pp. 345-351.